T0008635

An Irish Country Yuletide

By Patrick Taylor

An Irish Country Doctor
An Irish Country Village
An Irish Country Christmas
An Irish Country Girl
An Irish Country Courtship
A Dublin Student Doctor
An Irish Country Wedding
Fingal O'Reilly, Irish Doctor
The Wily O'Reilly: Irish Country Stories
An Irish Doctor in Peace and at War
An Irish Doctor in Love and at Sea
An Irish Country Love Story
An Irish Country Practice
An Irish Country Cottage
An Irish Country Family
An Irish Country Welcome
An Irish Country Yuletide

Only Wounded
Pray for Us Sinners
Now and in the Hour of Our Death

"Home Is the Sailor" (e-original)

An Irish Country Yuletide

PATRICK TAYLOR

A Tom Doherty Associates Book
New York

This is a work of fiction. All of the characters, organizations, and events portrayed in this novel are either products of the author's imagination or are used fictitiously.

AN IRISH COUNTRY YULETIDE

Maps by Elizabeth Danforth

A Forge Book
Published by Tom Doherty Associates
120 Broadway
New York, NY 10271

www.tor-forge.com

Forge® is a registered trademark of Macmillan Publishing Group, LLC.

The Library of Congress Cataloging-in-Publication Data
is available upon request.

ISBN 978-1-250-78090-4 (hardcover)
ISBN 978-1-250-78091-1 (ebook)

Our books may be purchased in bulk for promotional, educational, or business use. Please contact your local bookseller or the Macmillan Corporate and Premium Sales Department at 1-800-221-7945, extension 5442, or by email at MacmillanSpecialMarkets@macmillan.com.

First Edition: October 2021

Printed in the United States of America

0 9 8 7 6 5 4 3 2 1

To Dorothy

Acknowledgments

I would like to thank a large number of people, some of whom have worked with me from the beginning, and without whose unstinting help and encouragement I could not have written this series. They are:

In North America

Simon Hally, Carolyn Bateman, Tom Doherty, Paul Stevens, Kristin Sevick, Irene Gallo, Gregory Manchess, Patty Garcia, Alexis Saarela, Fleur Mathewson, Jamie Broadhurst, and Christina MacDonald, all of whom have contributed enormously to the literary and technical aspects of bringing this work from rough draft to bookshelf.

Natalia Aponte and Victoria Lea, my literary agents.

Don Kalancha and Joe Maier, who keep me right on contractual matters.

In the United Kingdom

Jessica and Rosie Buchman, my foreign rights agents.

To you all, Doctor Fingal Flahertie O'Reilly and I tender our most heartfelt gratitude and thanks.

Author's Note

You may be surprised, if you are familiar with the Irish Country Doctor series of novels, to see this shorter book, a novella, usually defined as a work of fiction between fifteen and forty thousand words. If you are not familiar with the series, I hope this novella has caught your attention, and if you enjoy it, may interest you in taking a look at the others.

And, in fact, it is not the first but the third shorter work I have essayed. The first was begun in 2007.

My wife and I were living in Ireland. My agent, Natalia Aponte, suggested I write a novella and she wondered about an Irish ghost story. I agreed, started the work, but found I could not tell the story in forty thousand words, and in short order it had become the full-length novel *An Irish Country Girl,* with young Maureen O'Hanlon as the central character. Maureen grew up to become Mrs. "Kinky" Kincaid, Doctor O'Reilly's widowed housekeeper. That work also explains why she is fey, endowed with the sight that gives her glimpses of the future. And if you are surprised that a man who spent the greater part of his career doing scientific research has no difficulty believing this, please let me quote a passage from the author's note in *An Irish Country Girl.*

"Some Irish women do have 'the sight.' My paternal grandmother did. How else could she have suddenly sat up in her chair and announced, 'Maggie's dead'? Her younger sister Maggie lived fifty miles away. Thirty minutes later the telephone rang to give us the news of Maggie's earlier demise, at almost exactly the time Granny had made her pronouncement."

Not only is Kinky fey, she is a marvelous cook and, as in all books in the series, some of her recipes appear in this work once the story is told. In 2017, her *Irish Country Cookbook* appeared with 150 more recipes, all written by my wife, Dorothy.

My next attempt to write a novella did succeed. *Home Is the Sailor,* describing Doctor Fingal O'Reilly's postwar return from service in the Royal Navy's battleship HMS *Warspite* to the make-believe village of Ballybucklebo, appeared in 2013 in ebook format only. In response to numerous requests to make it available in paper, the story was added to the hardback and later trade paper editions of *The Wily O'Reilly,* published in 2014. It is a bound collection of my medical humour columns, *Taylor's Twist,* that ran monthly for ten years in *Stitches: The Journal of Medical Humour.* It was here that the main characters of the Irish Country Doctor series first appeared.

And finally, the senior editor at Forge Books, Kristin Sevick, wondered aloud in October 2019 if I would give another novella a try. She thought Christmas in Ballybucklebo in 1965 would be a cheerful time and place in which to set it. She was right, and here it is.

Coming up with a title has proven a little tricky. *An Irish Country Christmas* was already taken. That was published in 2008. The phrase "Happy Holidays" is much in vogue in the twenty-first century, but in Ulster in the 1960s would have earned you a quizzical look and perhaps a remark that Ebenezer Scrooge was not visited by the spirits of Holidays Past, Present, and Yet to Come. It also meant that the title *A Christmas Carol. In Prose. Being a Ghost Story of Christmas,* commonly known as *A Christmas Carol,* was taken.

It is here I must pay special tribute to two remarkable women, my Ulster-born wife, Dorothy, and my personal editor, Carolyn Bateman.

Dorothy, after much thought, suggested, "You get lots of readers writing how much they enjoy the Irish history and folklore in your books. I think the title's there. Holly and mistletoe were sacred to the druids. We used them as Christmas decorations in Ulster in the '50s and '60s."

"I know. Young men kissed young women under the mistletoe."

Her smile was quite delicious, then she said, "Have you seen the Newgrange Celtic burial mound in County Meath?"

I shook my head.

"We had a school trip there when I was a girl. We were taught that it was built to celebrate the winter solstice on December 21 and for several days after—and that festival's name is still in use today. Yule or Yuletide."

"I think we have a title. *An Irish Country Yuletide.*"

A title for a work for which Carolyn Bateman must take a great deal of credit. My first book of fiction, a collection of short stories called *Only Wounded,* was published in 1997. Carolyn, a freelance editor, was chosen to edit this work. We have worked together ever since. When Kristin mooted the idea for a novella, Carolyn and I decided to put other projects aside and concentrate on this work. Because of her commitment we finished it in record time.

And before I go, I would like to thank some other people:

Ron Reznick, M.D., our friend and family physician who kept me right on the technical details of chickenpox, a disease that I have completely forgotten about—except for vague memories of my personal bout with it in 1972.

Doctor Fred Alexander was one year ahead of me at medical school. We became colleagues in the seventies when we worked together at the University of Calgary. We have kept in touch ever since. He was a pathologist and it is to him that I am indebted for affirming the accuracy of my description of leukaemia.

Doctors David and Sharon Mortimer, both doctors of philosophy, two outstanding pioneers in the field of human reproduction with whom I was privileged to work at the University of Calgary in the eighties, and with whom I have maintained a friendship to this day. Both Sharon, a native-born Australian, and David, courtesy of working for years in that country, speak fluent "Strine." They advised me on accuracy when an Australian character speaks in this work.

And when it comes to language, the English vernacular of Northern Ireland tends to stray from the *Oxford English Dictionary* and manuals of grammar and usage. For readers who might become confused, a glossary is appended on page 189.

And now, having made my explanations and given my thanks, I hope they will add to your enjoyment of this novella.

PATRICK TAYLOR
Saltspring Island
British Columbia
Canada
February 2020

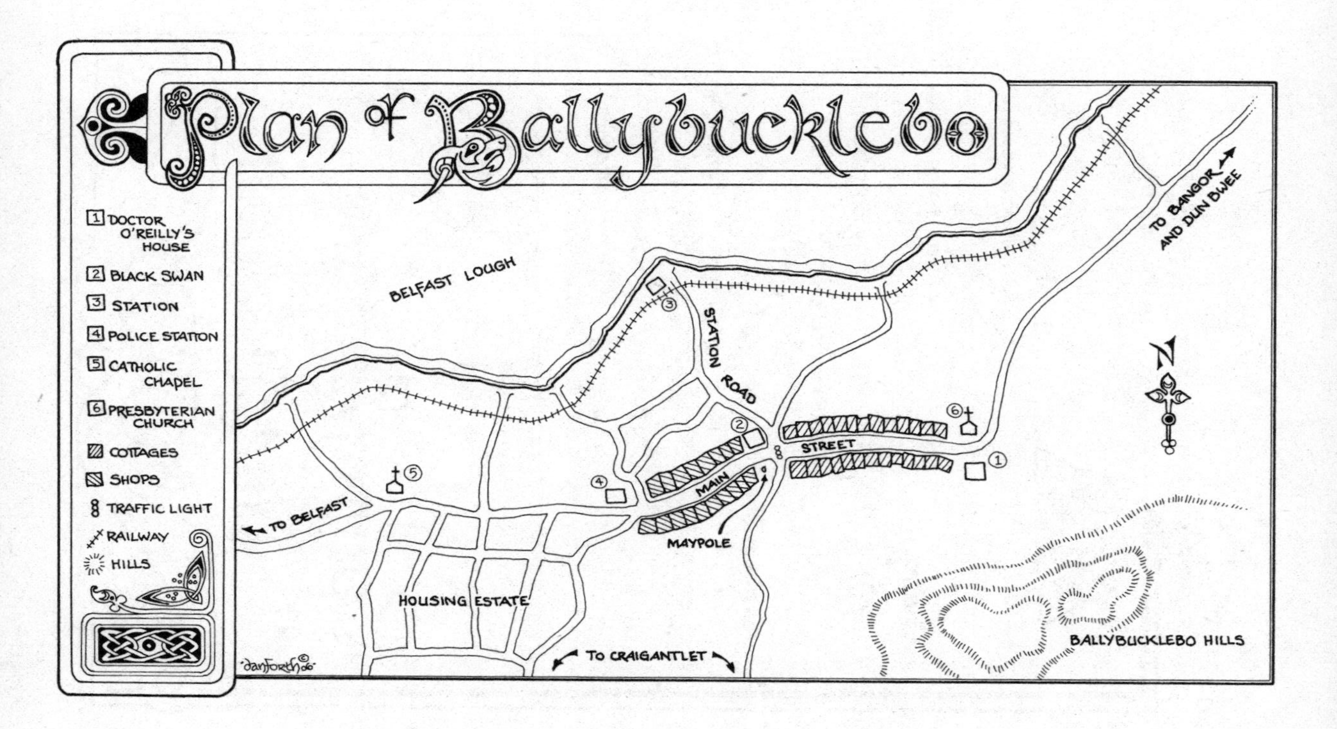
Plan of Ballybucklebo
1 DOCTOR O'REILLY'S HOUSE
2 BLACK SWAN
3 STATION
4 POLICE STATION
5 CATHOLIC CHAPEL
6 PRESBYTERIAN CHURCH
COTTAGES
SHOPS
TRAFFIC LIGHT
RAILWAY
HILLS
BELFAST LOUGH
STATION ROAD
MAIN STREET
MAYPOLE
HOUSING ESTATE
TO BELFAST
TO CRAIGANTLET
TO BANGOR AND DUN BWEE
BALLYBUCKLEBO HILLS
N
danforth © 06

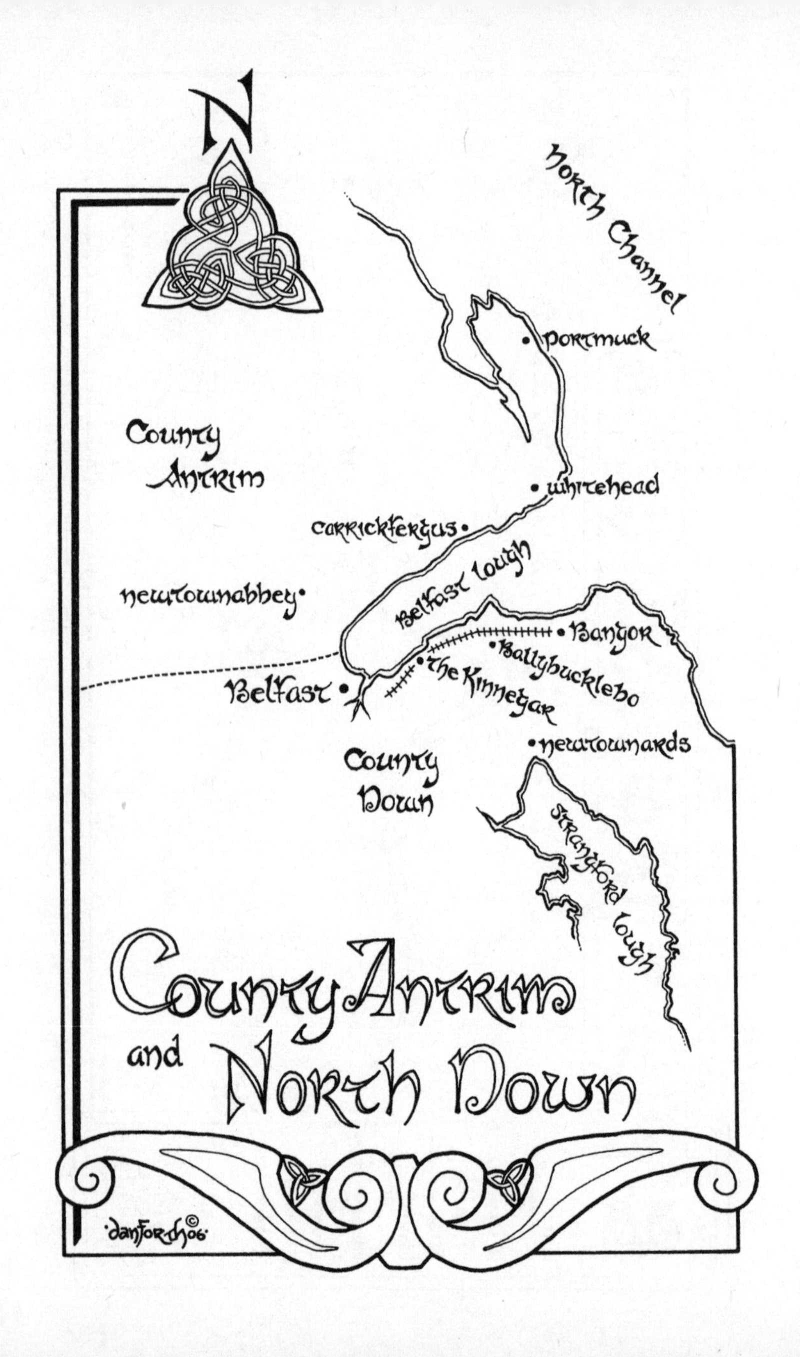
N
North Channel
Portmuck
County Antrim
Whitehead
Carrickfergus
Belfast Lough
Newtownabbey
Bangor
Ballyhucklebo
The Kinnegar
Belfast
Newtownards
County Down
Strangford Lough
County Antrim
and
North Down
·danforth 06·©

December 1965

1

Great Art O' Letter Writing

Doctor Fingal Flahertie O'Reilly tried to stifle a distinctly satisfied burp as he finished the last trace of his housekeeper's sherry trifle. "Sorry, Kitty," he said to his wife of nearly six months.

"You are forgiven." She smiled at him, and the sparkle in her grey-flecked-with-amber eyes, as always, made him tingle. Had done so ever since he'd met her as a student nurse in Sir Patrick Dun's Hospital in Dublin in 1934. They'd parted in 1936, he to pursue his, to him, all-important career, she to Tenerife in the Canary Islands to care for orphans of the Spanish Civil War.

Until last summer, he hadn't seen her since, but he'd carried an ember for the student nurse from Tallaght, Dublin, all his life. Even during his short marriage in 1940. That ember had woken and burst into flame when he, a widower for twenty-four years, had discovered she was working in Belfast's Royal Victoria Hospital as a senior nursing sister in the neurosurgical operating theatre.

Kitty leant to one side, stretched her right arm down, and straightened up holding something tied with a red ribbon. "Seeing Christmas Day will be here soon, I've brought you an early present."

"What are they?" he said, eying what he now saw was a bundle of envelopes.

"I'm still unpacking a few boxes from my Belfast flat and this morning I found these and thought you might enjoy reading them today."

"Why today?"

She smiled. "Because it's special. Our first Christmas as man and wife." She blew him a kiss.

The door to the dining room opened and Mrs. Kincaid, or "Kinky," as she was known, his housekeeper of nineteen years, entered carrying a tray with a steaming pot of coffee and an open box of Rowntree's After Eight dark chocolate mint cremes.

"Kinky, you have excelled yourself," O'Reilly said. "Prawn cocktail, roast leg of lamb with mint sauce, potatoes roasted in goose fat, broad beans, and carrots? You are a culinary genius."

She chuckled, making her silver chignon and three chins shake. "Sure, wasn't it only a shmall-little thing, so," she said in her offhand way, but he could tell she was pleased with the praise. "I see you've eaten up however little much was in it."

Her Cork accent was gentle on O'Reilly's ear.

"It's nothing less than you deserve, Doctor, and you, Mrs. O'Reilly. You work very hard the pair of you, helping other people, day in, day out. You deserve good food when you come home, so. Now, here does be your coffee and After Eights." She set the tray on the table, unloaded its contents, and cleared away the dirty plates. "I know you're expecting the marquis in a few minutes, so when he arrives, I'll take him up to the lounge and bring the coffee and mints up once you're all settled." She fixed O'Reilly with a steely gaze. "Do not, sir. Do not eat all of them."

O'Reilly cringed just a little at his housekeeper's no-nonsense tone. "I promise." Those citizens of Ballybucklebo who knew their middle-aged medical advisor as gruff and taciturn would have been amazed by his humility. But she'd always had that effect on him whenever she admonished him. He'd met Kinky here in this very house in 1938, just before he'd gone off to the war, and had returned here to buy the practice in 1946.

The housekeeper left, closing the door behind her. As she went, a sudden gust hurled rain against the room's bow window making a noise like a badly uncoordinated kettle drummer.

"Glad we're in here tonight," O'Reilly said. "Heaven help the sailors. That's a powerful wind." He shook his head, offered Kitty a mint chocolate, and helped himself to two wrapped in their open-ended paper envelopes. "Speaking of power, as her fellow Cork folk would say, 'That Maureen "Kinky" Kincaid is a powerful woman, so.'" He bit into a bittersweet mint. Perfection. "I'd have been lost without her these nineteen years. Back then for her sake I'd hoped she might remarry, but for my own, I don't know what I'd have done without her. Now with you here, love, I'm not a domestically useless old bachelor anymore, and when she told us she was getting married again, I couldn't have been more delighted. I suppose I'm selfish, but I'm very glad she stayed on with me for as long as she did."

"You? Selfish, old bear?" Kitty finished her mint. "I know you too well. It's all part of the—put that third mint down, Fingal."

He set it back in the box.

"Do you remember that 1950s song, 'The Great Pretender'?"

"Yes. The Platters wasn't it, 1955?"

She nodded. "That's you in a nutshell. Stiff upper lip. Terrified of letting your feelings show."

"Well. I, that is. I mean . . ." But it was true. He often felt things deeply inside but had great difficulty saying the words aloud.

"Rubbish." She smiled to show there was no anger in her,

picked up her early gift, and handed it to him. "And I've got proof of your feelings in writing. Have a read of some of these."

He accepted the bundle and recognised his own straggling scrawl on the top envelope: Miss Kitty O'Hallorhan, 10A, Wellington Park, Belfast. His breath caught. She'd kept the letters he'd written to her after they'd met again in August 1964. Too scared of being rejected face-to-face, he'd taken to expressing his true feelings in letters. He inhaled deeply.

"You kept them, even after we were married?"

She blew him a kiss. "Of course, I did. Some of them are very sweet, Fingal. You were and still are a very romantic man, and I love you."

He rose, leaving the bundle on the table and intending to give her a kiss, but the front doorbell rang.

"That'll be the marquis. Let's greet him." Kitty rose and as they left the room, she sang out. "We're answering the door, Kinky."

Lord John MacNeill stood on the step of Number One Main, Ballybucklebo, his camelhair coat sodden, his trilby hat dripping with rain, looking very much like a man in need of a friend. He and O'Reilly had got to know each other years ago through their shared interest in the game of rugby and the Ballybucklebo Bonnaughts Sports Club.

"Come in out of that, John. I'm sure the geese are flying backward."

"Thanks, Fingal." John MacNeill came in from the howling gale and shut the door behind him. "Hello, Kitty."

"Hello, John. My goodness, you look wet through."

Kinky, who had always had a soft spot for the marquis, had come to the door anyway. Now she curtseyed, and said, "Let me take your hat and coat, sir. The wires must be shaking out there, so."

"It is a dirty night." He handed her his sopping coat and hat, revealing a head of neatly brushed iron-grey hair.

"I'll take these through to my kitchen," she said, "and put them to dry in front of the range then I'll bring up the coffee."

"Thank you, Mrs. Kincaid. That is very kind."

She made another curtsey and left.

"Come up to the fire, John," O'Reilly said. "You must be foundered."

"Mmm." He rubbed his hands together. "Trifle nippy. Please lead on."

As they crossed the first landing, the marquis nodded to the photograph of O'Reilly's old battleship, HMS *Warspite*. "Saw the *Times* yesterday. Historical piece. I didn't know, but seems they finished scrapping her in 1957."

"She ran aground ten years before in Prussia Cove, Cornwall, on her way to the breaker's yard." O'Reilly laughed. "The grand old lady always did have a mind of her own." He and Kitty stood aside to let John MacNeill precede them into the cosy upstairs lounge where the curtains were closed over the bay windows and a coal fire burned in the grate. There, presumably under some kind of truce, O'Reilly's white cat Lady Macbeth lay curled up beside his black Labrador, Arthur Guinness.

Her ladyship ignored them. Arthur opened one brown eye, smiled at the newcomer, and thumped his tail down—once.

"Have a pew, John." O'Reilly indicated a semicircle of four armchairs arranged around the fire.

Kitty took a chair and John sat beside her, crossing his legs and hitching up his flannel trouser leg to protect the crease.

Kinky appeared and set the coffee and mints on a table beside the fire as O'Reilly stood by the sideboard. "Thanks, Kinky," he said as she left. "My love?"

"Have we some Taylor's port still?"

O'Reilly nodded. "John?"

"Same as you, Fingal, as always."

In moments Kitty had her port, the men their neat John Jameson Irish whiskey, and O'Reilly had seated himself beside John MacNeill. "Cheers."

"Cheers." They drank.

"So, John. You sounded a bit—well—not entirely yourself on the phone. What can we do?"

John MacNeill stared at the carpet for what seemed like ages until he raised his head and looked O'Reilly in the eye. "It's my brother in Australia."

O'Reilly choked on his whiskey, coughing and spluttering, "Brother? What brother? John, I didn't know you had a brother. How could I not know?"

John's smile was wry. "Not many people do, and the rest of the family would be quite happy if no one did. Father was adamant that people not speak of Andrew and it's a measure of how much my father was respected—or feared—that no one did."

O'Reilly leant forward in his seat, ignoring his whiskey. "Why ever not?"

John sipped his drink. "Andrew MacNeill was only two years younger than me, but in some ways, he was younger than that. I took him under my wing when we were children. Especially for the three years we were at Harrow together. MacNeill major and MacNeill minor they called us. I protected him from the inevitable bullying. Kept an eye on him as long as I could. He was sixteen when I left Harrow in 1919. I didn't learn until after he'd been sent down from Cambridge in 1925 with a rowing blue, but no degree, that he had become a complete scoundrel. The usual culprits I'm afraid—drinking, gambling, a rather racy taste in women. By then, I was within weeks of finishing at Sandhurst officer's training school."

O'Reilly shook his head.

John set his glass on the table. "Then, in mid-1926, Andrew was expelled from White's club in Piccadilly." He glanced up and saw Kitty's questioning look.

"It's the oldest gentlemen's club in London. Founded in 1693. Very exclusive. Very proper. Very."

There was a short silence until O'Reilly said, "This must be difficult for you to talk about, John. Take your time."

"Thank you, Fingal." He uncrossed and recrossed his legs.

"I tried to help him. He was my little brother and I loved him. But he wouldn't accept my help. Would never be serious long enough to discuss anything. I never found out why he was thrown out of White's. Father refused to talk about it. He was a reasonably patient man, my father. He'd survived the shame of Andrew being sent down. Willing to let a young man go through a bit of a wild period. But the business at White's, well, it was the last straw for the old man. So, Father paid off Andrew's gambling debts and settled an out-of-wedlock paternity suit." The marquis shook his head.

O'Reilly said, "And you probably still feel guilty about not being able to help him."

"I do." John nodded. "I know, Fingal, you've read Somerset Maugham's pre-war South Pacific short stories. I've seen them sitting in this very room. One of his stock characters was the upper-class waster who was provided with a monthly stipend remitted to a local bank in one of the distant colonies on condition he never came home. The remittance man.

"Andrew was one. Father packed him off to Australia, gave

him a monthly allowance sent to a bank in Perth, and told my brother never to show his face in Ireland again."

"How awful. For both of you," Kitty said.

John grimaced. "It was. I missed Andrew, but the war kept me occupied for some time. I stayed in the Guards until 1951, then I had to come back to run the estate after Father's death."

"Of course."

"I thought we'd never hear from Andrew again, but I got a letter in June of '51 shortly after Father's death."

O'Reilly thought immediately of his letters sitting in the dining room, but he turned his attention back to John MacNeill. "The letter, sending his condolences for Father's death and asking me to cancel his allowance, contained a clipping from the *County Down Spectator* about the Ballybucklebo Bonnaughts seeking donations to improve their clubhouse. Someone here must have stayed in touch with him and sent him the paper. In the letter, Andrew claimed to have made a great deal of money in gold mining and asked for the privilege of meeting half the costs of the clubhouse renovations. Anonymously, of course. There was only a PO box address from a place called Kalgoorlie in Western Australia."

"Good gracious. So, he was still in Australia twenty-five years later," Kitty said.

"He was. And a rich man."

O'Reilly asked, "And was the promise honoured?"

"After some back and forth correspondence, indeed it was. Although I made it clear this was an anonymous donation, I'm afraid most people at the time suspected my father was their benefactor, and I couldn't correct them."

"I certainly thought it was your father," said Fingal.

"I wrote Andrew a number of personal letters in care of the address in Kalgoorlie asking him to come home, but never received any reply. Indeed, those letters about the clubhouse were the last we'd heard until two days ago." He sat back in his chair and picked up his glass but didn't drink.

Lady Macbeth stood, arched her back, then trotted to Kitty, jumped up onto her lap, and began dough-punching, alternately pushing and withdrawing one front paw then the other against Kitty's thighs.

She stroked the little cat, whose purrs rumbled gently, and looked at O'Reilly. He wanted to jump into the conversation, to ask outright what had happened next. But one look at John told him the man had to tell this in his own time. So, O'Reilly diverted himself by sipping his whiskey, taking a long deep breath, and listening to the rattle of the rain on the window.

"Two days ago, I got a long-distance call from someone purporting to be Andrew and I'm damn sure it was. I'd know that voice anywhere. Said he was ill, that he'd booked flights to Heathrow arriving on Thursday the sixteenth. He'll overnight there, fly to Aldergrove, and arrive in Ulster on Friday the seventeenth. He wants to see his old home one more time, he said, and wondered if he might also be able to see the clubhouse."

"One more time," O'Reilly said.

"Yes, that's how he put it. It doesn't sound good, I'm afraid. I fear the worst." John ran a hand through his hair and looked down to the ground.

"And of course, you said yes, John?" Kitty spoke gently.

"Naturally. He can stay with Myrna and me at the house."

O'Reilly watched as John again raked a hand through his hair. "You know how strong-willed my sister can be. She had very little empathy for him then. I hope she will have more now." He paused. "I'll hire a private nurse if he needs one. But perhaps, if he's well enough . . ." He paused and cleared his throat. "Perhaps

I can put on a little thank-you for him at the club." He shrugged, raising his hands palms up. "What do you think, Fingal?"

O'Reilly frowned. "I'll come and see him on Sunday. I know he'll be jet-lagged, but if he's fit enough, why not bring him to the club's annual Christmas party on Wednesday the twenty-second. Let the rest of the executive know in advance, of course, and simply introduce him to the folks in attendance? If that would be all right with your brother?"

John frowned, stroked his chin, then smiled. "I think that would be a splendid idea. Andrew's always loved a party from the time he was a small child. But he's not under the National Health Service, so send me a bill."

O'Reilly snorted. "Send you a bill? To do a friend's long-lost brother a small favour?" He shook his head. "In the words of one of the locals, 'My esteemed gracious lord—away off and chase yourself.'"

John MacNeill smiled. "Thanks, to you both, for listening and thank you, Fingal, for your sage advice. I will be happy to accept your offer of your medical services and I'll have a word with the rest of the executive so Andrew will be welcomed properly." He finished his whiskey, refused a second, rose, and said, "Now I must be trotting along."

"I'll see you out," O'Reilly said, "and I'll be a minute or two, Kitty. There's something I'd like to read downstairs."

"Good night, John. It's lovely to see you and I do so hope your brother's illness isn't serious. Please say hello to Myrna."

"Thank you, Kitty. And I will."

"And, Fingal . . ." She smiled, and her right eyebrow rose in that enticingly provocative gesture he had always loved. "Take all the time you need with your reading. I've got Lady Macbeth for company and my *The Spy Who Came in from the Cold* to finish."

Having shown John MacNeill out into the gale, O'Reilly closed the front door and locked it. Good God, O'Reilly thought. John MacNeill and he had been close friends since 1946. And as John and Myrna's medical advisor, O'Reilly had thought he knew just about everything there was to know about the MacNeill family. It certainly was going to take some unravelling—but then Fingal O'Reilly had always enjoyed mysteries.

In moments he was at the dining room table holding the bundle of letters, undoing their red ribbon, and riffling through them. He soon established by the postmarks that they were in chronological order, so, he thought, in the words of Julie Andrews in this year's film *The Sound of Music,* "Let's start at the very beginning."

He opened the first envelope, drew out three pages of notepaper, and began to read. He noted he'd dated it September 12, 1964.

Dear Kitty,

I had great difficulty believing it in August when Barry told me a Sister Caitlin O'Hallorhan was working in the Royal and wished to be remembered to me. Remembered? Since I let you go in 1936, I have never forgotten you and to see you last night, hear your voice, kiss you good night, filled my soul.

He'd tried to tell her then, but the words simply had not come until he had sat at his desk and penned these words the next day.

Today I took Arthur Guinness for a walk and on our way, I saw a familiar tree. A Japanese maple. It is a delicate tree with lissome boughs and multi-fingered leaves. I care deeply for that little tree.

I love its annual cycle and think of it as a reflecting glass for my own feelings.

In the winter the tree is dormant, its bony fingers knobbed with knuckles. It's a time of sleeping, when all creation turns into itself, and the world passes by unheeded, simply to be lived through until spring.

In my spring I met you, a golden girl.

Fingal had to stop reading and blow his nose.

We fell in love, a love so gentle, so fumbling and inchoate we hardly understood it. It was a love that, like the maple's buds, swelled, burst, and flourished—and might have been consummated but for a sudden late frost. My love, like a frozen leaf, lay curled on the unforgiving ground.

The dead leaf cannot know that the tree survives. I didn't know you held within you the tiny buds of our love, which you would nourish and keep alive to await a new spring.

What tells the maple buds to grow once winter has passed? I do not know what kismet put me face-to-face with you last month. I do know that meeting made my love grow again. I tried to blight it, to tell it I was snow-blind. But I could no more stop loving you than the tree could stop its spring growth.

After ripening, buds must burst. When I kissed you last night, I felt myself stretched by the burgeoning growth within. When you took your courage and told me you still loved me, my own love, which had stayed quietly curled in on itself, shook loose and, like a new leaf, opened and smiled at the sun.

But this mature, full-blooded love is far from the simple green love of the past.

The ripe leaves of my maple today are full, and their weight bends the boughs. They are red, somewhere between copper and maroon, a colour that would take the skills of a painter in oils to capture, and with more accuracy than these poor words of a physician. Their beauty stops my breath in my throat just like the beauty of our love holds a warm hand round my heart.

Before long they will start to fall to make a carpet of fire, but their deaths will not be the death of my tree. My tree will bide and hold its secret into itself, ready when the time comes to flourish again in spring sun. Then its leaves will burst forth as will my love . . . now and forever.

Your loving Fingal

Fingal blew his nose again, folded the pages, slipped the letter into the envelope, and put it to the bottom of the pile.

He stood slowly, walked across to his surgery, and put the bundle into the one drawer of the old roll-top desk he kept locked. He'd savour his thoughts about the rest, which he would read at his leisure.

He glanced up and grinned. Now he'd go upstairs, kiss his golden girl, and tell her how much he loved her.

2

Never Make Long Visits

"Barry." A surprised but smiling Fingal O'Reilly opened the front door wider. Faint December afternoon sunbeams crept over the doorstep as if embarrassed by their failure to show up yesterday. "By God, it's good to see you, and you've brought the sun with you." He offered his hand and they shook. "Damn sight better day than yesterday." He hadn't seen the young doctor since he'd popped in one late October morning on his way to visit his folks in Ballyholme. O'Reilly wondered what the lad might want, turning up unannounced like this. "Come in, come in."

"Thanks, Fingal. Good to be back in Number One Main Street again. I've missed the place." From July 1964 to June the following year, Doctor Barry Laverty had been O'Reilly's assistant with a view to partnership, but had left to spend the last six months of that year as a trainee obstetrician/gynaecologist in Ballymena's Waveney Hospital. O'Reilly had accepted his choice with resignation, thinking, well, that's it then. Another young doctor lost to specialization. But two months ago, Barry had phoned O'Reilly to ask if the offer to rejoin his practice in January '66 still stood.

O'Reilly, with great pleasure, had assured him the position was his for the asking.

Barry would complete the training but had decided specialization was not for him. He had given the hospital the two months' notice it required.

O'Reilly closed the door. "I wasn't expecting you until January first. What brings you here today?"

"Well, I—"

"Let's sit down. Come into the surgery."

Once the two men had settled themselves, O'Reilly behind his desk, Barry as always, sitting on the examining couch, O'Reilly said, "So, tell me what's up?"

"Professor Dunseath at Queens University phoned me a couple of days ago, told me that finding junior staff for a country hospital had been tricky in the middle of the hospital year. There were no local candidates, so he'd advertised in the *British Medical Journal* and recently had an application from Lagos, Nigeria, for my post. It had taken a while to look into the man's credentials, but everything was in order.

"As it turns out, Doctor Tunge Omolokum is arriving tomorrow to get settled into his new home."

"Ulster's a brave way from home for him. And the man needs a place to live?"

"Exactly. Would I consider taking the last two weeks of December as holiday with pay so the new man could go straight from Aldergrove airport to the junior doctors' quarters in the Waveney?" Barry grinned. "It wasn't a difficult decision."

O'Reilly laughed. "I'm sure you'll not mind a bit of extra time off."

"Not at all, but I'm bit of a waif and stray. Of no fixed abode. When the prof asked me on Tuesday to vacate my quarters by today, Thursday, I phoned Mum. She's happy to have me for as long as I need a roof, but I did want to be absolutely sure I could move back in here on January first." Barry grinned. "That is, if it's all right with the new Mrs. O'Reilly."

"As soon as we heard you wanted to come back, Kitty said of course you could have your attic back. And it'll only be for a few months."

"Oh?" Barry sounded disappointed.

"It's all right. We're not chucking you out. You know the milkman, Archie Auchinleck, proposed to Kinky. They got engaged on the fourth of December and are getting wed in April. She'll be moving in with Archie so you can have her old quarters."

Big smile. "That's terrific, Fingal. Archie is a very lucky man. And so am I. I'll be here at nine o'clock January first. Now, I'm on my way to my folks' place in Ballyholme so I'd best be running along. I just thought I'd stop to say hello, check on my room, and pay you the compliments of the season."

"And a merry Christmas to you too, Barry." O'Reilly nodded to himself and thought, the answer will probably be no, but it's worth a try. He tilted his head to one side. "I really shouldn't ask you this, but I don't suppose there's any chance you'd be able to give me a hand before January first? I'm still single-handed, and we're in the middle of a Europe-wide chickenpox pandemic."

Barry frowned, scratched his blond hair, and smoothed down a tuft that always stuck up. "Gosh, Mum's really looking forward to having her boy home for a while and I could use the break."

O'Reilly swallowed his disappointment.

Barry nodded to himself, then a slow smile started. It was his turn to cock his head and look at his old boss. "You do look a bit tired, Fingal. I won't lie, the extra bit of spondulix, as Donal would say, will come in handy." He paused. "How would it work if I take the home visits and emergencies tomorrow? I'd have to sleep here tomorrow night. The next morning's Saturday, so no surgery. I'll go home to Ballyholme and I'm sorry, Fingal, but I'll stick you with weekend call."

"That's perfectly all right. We can work out the rota on Monday for the rest of December, and for when you officially rejoin on New Year's Day." O'Reilly clapped Barry on the back. "This is manna from heaven," he said with a broad grin.

Barry, who'd always been a little shy, coloured. "I'll have to explain to Mum, but if she's all right with that I could start tomorrow. I'll phone you when I've spoken to her."

O'Reilly could see the man was steeling himself to ask for something more.

The words came out in a rush. "But I'd like Christmas Day off to spend in Ballyholme. And a few days in January to write the papers and sit the orals for my Diploma of the Royal College of Ob/Gyn. It doesn't mean I'm a specialist, but it will say I've had extra training."

Young Barry Laverty was maturing, O'Reilly thought. He'd never have dared ask for things like that last year. Good for him. And the extra qualification in obstetrics and gynaecology wouldn't hurt the practice either. "I've contingency plans for cover on the twenty-second, the day of the Sports Club's Christmas party, and for Christmas Day. So, we'll both have it off—but I want you to agree to pop in on our at-home on Christmas morning with your mum and dad and promise to pass the exams in January."

"I think I can promise for the first. We'll have to see about the second."

"Fair enough. Your old attic quarters are as you left them, but we'll have to ask Kinky if they're what the housing inspectors call 'fit for human habitation.' Let's go and talk to her." He headed off, followed by Barry, along the hall, leaving the surgery and the empty waiting room. O'Reilly, like most Ulster GPs, ran his practice from his home.

The kitchen was warm from the heat of the Aga range and redolent of ginger from several dozen freshly baked ginger crisp biscuits and a tray of gingerbread men cooling on baking racks on a kitchen shelf. Kinky had her back to the men, but O'Reilly knew she was stuffing dates with marzipan, a traditional treat if friends dropped in for a pre-Christmas drink.

She turned and started. Her agate eyes glared, and she shook an index finger at O'Reilly. "How often, Doctor dear, have I asked you not to creep up on me like that? A body after such a shock could, as they say here in the Wee North, take the rickets, so."

"Sorry, Kinky, but see what the cat dragged in."

Kinky put her hands on her hips, took two steps forward, and enveloped Barry in a huge hug. "It's like the return of the prodigal son, although we're a bit short of fatted calves. It does be a great pleasure to see you, *a chara*." She turned to O'Reilly and said sternly, "Lady Macbeth is too shmall a cat to have tackled Doctor Laverty." Then she turned back to Barry. "Welcome back, sir."

"Thanks, Kinky. And congratulations on your engagement."

Kinky looked down at the floor and said shyly, "Well, thank you, sir. Archie does be a good man, so."

"Now, Kinky, we need your advice." A request like that was the surest way to get Maureen "Kinky" Kincaid, née O'Hanlon and soon to be Auchinleck, on side. "You know Doctor Laverty is coming back to us in January?"

"I do, so. And I do be very pleased."

"He's agreed to help out for the next two weeks with this chickenpox outbreak, so he'll need somewhere to sleep when he's on call, starting tomorrow."

"Well then, it's dusted and hoovered, but the room will want airing-out and fresh sheets on the bed. I've finished with the dates, so I think I'll go do the room now. Are you staying for a visit, Doctor Laverty? If you are, why don't you both go upstairs and I'll bring you up a pot of tea and a plate of these fresh ginger crisps for you to enjoy while I attend to your room, so." She started to fill the kettle with water but when neither man moved, she stopped and turned to them. "Well, what are you waiting for? You'll not get a better offer than that."

"Have you time, Barry?" said O'Reilly. "Kinky's ginger crisps are famous and it would be good to catch up."

Barry smiled broadly. "Why not?"

"Well then, run along, Doctors, and let me get on with my work. The fire's lit so it'll be cosy, and I'll be along in two shakes of a duck's tail."

As they came to the foot of the staircase, Barry said, "May I phone Mum, Fingal? Explain I'm going to be a bit later than I'd told her. I'll tell them about my change in plans when I get home."

"Go right ahead." O'Reilly pointed to the wall-mounted phone then turned and headed upstairs to the lounge. The fire was mostly embers, so he stirred them with a poker, making sparks fly up the chimney, and chucked on a shovelful of coal from the scuttle. "That's better," he said to himself, lowering his bulk into one of the armchairs. He picked up his copy of *Hawaii* by James Michener. He had got to the bit where the measles epidemic was starting in the 1850s.

It eventually killed 20 percent of the native population who had no natural immunity. Europeans do have some natural resistance, he thought, and we've had a vaccine since 1963. Bloody good thing too. He yawned. Pity there was no chickenpox vaccine yet. It was an insidious disease and could have alarming complications.

Kinky, hotly pursued by Barry, appeared. Barry held back until Kinky had set the tray on the coffee table.

"Thanks, Kinky. Have a pew, Barry." O'Reilly marked his place and put his book on the table.

Kinky withdrew, saying, "I'll see to your quarters now, Doctor Laverty."

"Thanks, Kinky." Barry sat. "And Mum said thanks for letting her know and sends her best wishes."

"Good." O'Reilly poured two cups. "Here. Help yourself to milk and sugar. And do have a go at these ginger biscuits." He snaffled two and set them in his saucer. "So," said O'Reilly, "you decided against ob/gyn?"

"I did and it didn't take long. I grant you obstetrics is probably the happiest speciality. Babies bring their own welcomes, but I wasn't so interested in gynaecology." He took a bite from a biscuit. "Mmm. Delicious. And it's not like general practice. I learnt it from you, I think, but I honestly enjoy getting to know our patients well, feeling part of the local community."

"You've been following in my footsteps. I spent a year in the thirties at the Rotunda Maternity Hospital in Dublin. I left for the same reasons. And very glad I did too. How else could I have met characters like our arch trickster Donal Donnelly?"

"Or a strange old bird like Maggie MacCorkle with headaches above the crown of her head?"

Both men laughed and O'Reilly helped himself to two more ginger biscuits.

Barry said with a cheeky grin, "And like your honourable self, Doctor O'Reilly, I'd become very fond of Kinky's cooking and am looking forward to it again." He inclined his head in the direction of O'Reilly's waistline.

"Impudent pup," O'Reilly said, but he smiled.

"Ah," said Barry. "'But good men starve for want of impudence.'"

"Dryden," O'Reilly said, "*Epilogue to Constantine the Great*." He shook with laughter. "God," he said, "but I've missed our dueling quotations game." He rose. "Stand up."

Barry obeyed and O'Reilly did what, among Ulstermen—who never showed emotions in public—was unthinkable. He gave Barry an enormous hug. "I've missed you, my boy. Welcome back."

They separated. "Thank you, Fingal. It's good to be back. Very good."

O'Reilly thought back to Kinky's remark about the prodigal son. Nothing prodigal about Barry, but he was beginning to become the son O'Reilly had never had.

Kinky stuck her head round the door. "Your attic bedroom does be ready, so. You can move in whenever you like, Doctor Laverty."

"Thanks, Kinky."

"And now I'll go down and finish my preparations for your and Mrs. O'Reilly's dinner, sir." Kinky left.

Both men settled back into their chairs and sat in silence for a moment, the only sound the crack and pop of the coal fire and the crunching of ginger crisps. "Barry, do you mind if I ask you a personal question?"

Barry shook his head. "Fire away."

"I'm a bit surprised you've agreed to come back to work early. Would you tell me why? Not this nonsense about me looking tired and you needing the money."

Barry grinned. "I could tell you I'd been pining for your company, Fingal, but you'd not believe me."

"I would not." O'Reilly's shoulders shook.

"Do you remember a certain copper-haired, green-eyed school mistress?"

"Sue Nolan from Broughshane? Lovely girl." Barry and she had been an item earlier in the year but had fallen out over politics, a stupid reason to fall out in O'Reilly's opinion.

"Sue and I are back together, and this Christmas her folks are off to see her dad's brother in Philadelphia for two weeks. There's not much to do on the farm in December and the Nolans' nearest neighbour's son, Michael Alexander, he'll look after the beasts for them . . ."

"And, let me guess. When you told her you'd be coming back north to County Down, your Sue decided to spend her holidays in her flat in Holywood."

"She did—with her bone-headed springer spaniel, Max." Barry shifted in his seat. "It's only minutes from here. Much closer than Ballyholme."

"Fair play to you, Barry. And it's usually Kinky, but there's always someone here to answer the phone. You could even spend your on-call evenings with Sue. Sound good?"

"It does, Fingal. Very much. I was hoping that would work. And," he said shyly, "I am saving my money."

"Say no more. I'm delighted you and Sue are back together."

"So am I." Barry finished his tea and biscuit and rose.

"Thanks for the tea. Now I'd best be getting on home to Mum, and—"

O'Reilly heard the front door open and close. "That'll be Kitty home from the hospital." He finished his tea. "Let me give you a bit of advice before you go, Barry." O'Reilly often hid behind flippancy, but this time his voice was level and serious. "When you find the right woman, never let her go."

3

Rubbing the Poor Itch

Barry parked his elderly Volkswagen, which his mum, an avid fan of Wagner's Ring cycle, had named Brünnhilde. God bless Mum, she'd not been upset last night when he'd explained his plans to help out O'Reilly. And if she suspected that Sue's proximity had had a part to play in his decision to start early at Number One Main, she'd kept it to herself.

Across the road an isolated thatched cottage lay between the Belfast to Bangor railway line and the seashore. Barry got out into the bright but nippy day, lifted his bag from the back of the car, and paused to admire the view across a narrow marram grass–covered dune that shelved down to a sandy shore. The ebbing tide had washed the beach's face and the light breeze was drying it. The hills of Antrim rose hazily on the far shore of Belfast Lough. He took a deep breath of the sea's tang. He'd missed the ocean when he'd been living in Ballymena.

He crossed the road noticing curls of smoke coming from the cottage's chimney and relished another smell he'd missed—burning peat on the cold air. This was his last of four home visits to patients who has asked for them on this Friday morning. He took another deep and satisfying breath. The day had been busy—a surgical follow-up, a case of acute bronchitis, and yet another victim of the chickenpox pandemic. Still, it was a leisurely pace compared to his days stuck on the wards at Waveney Hospital.

Barry lifted the wrinkled trunk of a brass door knocker shaped like an elephant's head and knocked.

The door was opened by a young woman wearing an Aran sweater over navy blue trousers. Her shoulder-length red hair was uncombed, and she looked weary and anxious. "Yes?" she snapped, then looked down at his medical bag.

Barry smiled. "Mrs. Driscoll?"

"Aye. You must be the doctor?"

"I am. Doctor Laverty. Doctor O'Reilly's assistant. We got your request for a home visit. I worked here for a year six months ago and I've come back to rejoin the practice."

"Come in, then. You look young for a doctor, but it's glad I am to see you, sir. I'm new here, from County Cork, so. From Bandon."

There was nostalgia in her voice, but she managed to smile. She had the very same lilt to her voice that Kinky had and as he looked at her oval face, blue eyes, and light dusting of freckles, he thought of what Kinky might have looked like as a young woman in her mid-twenties.

She closed the front door. "It's my wee Jill. She's been ailing since Monday. I thought it was just a cold so I used my granny's cure, the yolk of a new-laid egg, six spoonfuls of red rosewater beaten together and sweetened with white sugar to be taken at bedtime for six nights—but it's been doing her no good at all, so. Then she broke out in a rash on Wednesday."

Barry could tell the woman was close to tears. "It sounds like your Jill is another victim of the chickenpox that's spreading like wildfire. It's usually a mild disease—" He stopped short. He wouldn't tell her how some cases could go on to develop into meningoencephalitis, infection of the membranes surrounding and the brain itself with serious consequences. Not many, but it did happen.

"Och, the poor wee mite. She's only six and far from home and it's all my own fault." She blew her nose with a delicate lacy handkerchief and continued briskly. "I hope it's only chickenpox, sir, indeed I do. I've her in the front room by the fire, but let me take your overcoat before we go in."

Barry shed his coat and Mrs. Driscoll hung it on a coat stand.

A few tears slipped down her cheeks and she dashed them away. "Her daddy and me, well, we're living apart right now and I've come north."

All the way from Cork? The whole length of Ireland? He looked around the cosy cottage and at the young woman in front of him, but said nothing.

"I've hardly slept since she took bad and I'm at my wit's end. We know no one here and being from the Republic, I'm not on the National Health."

"Don't worry about that now. I'll do my best for your daughter."

"Thank you, Doctor. This way." She led him along a hall with an uneven stone floor laid with woven rugs.

She stepped aside to let Barry into a comfortable room where a turf fire burned in a fireplace set into a fieldstone wall. The occasional wisp of smoke failed to make its way into the flue, but soon rose to the ceiling and was dissipated.

She moved to a settee where a blue-eyed little girl, red-haired like her mother, lay under a beige wool blanket, bright pink mittens on her hands. "Jill, this is Doctor Laverty. He's come for to make you all better, so."

As Barry knelt beside her he noticed the small, fluid-filled blisters on her forehead. They had been painted with pink calamine lotion. "Hello, Jill. How are you?"

"I had a headache. It's gone away, but Mammy says I've still to wear these silly mittens. To stop me scratching. And to stay in the house." She gulped and tears started. "Are you here to say the same thing? I don't want to talk to you." She turned her face away.

Barry rose and stood aside to let Mrs. Driscoll sit on the settee and hold her daughter. "Jill and I are supposed to be going to Robinson and Cleaver's in Belfast to see Santa Claus tomorrow."

Barry heard a heavy sniff.

"But I don't think we'll be able to go—"

More sniffling.

"—with her so sick. That rash turned to itchy blisters by teatime on Wednesday."

"You're describing the usual course of chickenpox," Barry said.

"I am?" She stared at her daughter's rash-stricken face. "Granny had a cure for," she mouthed, "the scars from it."

Jill's tears had stopped.

"And the calamine lotion we've been using helps the itch, doesn't it?"

"Yes, Mammy, and I try very, very," the second "very" was accompanied by a vigorous head nod, "hard not to scratch."

"Granny told everyone with any rash not to scratch and if it was needed when they got better, she used ashes of burnt rushes and gunpowder made up in hog lard."

"Ooooh," Jill said, "sounds yucky. I don't want you to put that on my face."

"Don't worry, pet, I won't. Mammy and nice Doctor Laverty are going to look after you, aren't we?"

"We are," Barry said. He did not want to sound critical but

felt duty-bound to enquire. "And you didn't take Jill to the surgery or ask Doctor O'Reilly for a visit?"

She shook her head. "With us from the Republic? I waited until this morning before I did ask."

He understood her reticence. Her medical care would not be state subsidised here in the North. "Don't worry about having to pay," Barry said. "I'll not be charging you." He was happy to be working once again with a senior colleague who always had encouraged Barry to do the right thing.

"You won't?" She took hold of his hand and quickly kissed the back of it. "Thank you, sir. Thank you."

Barry was embarrassed by her thanks and looked away.

A small voice said, "I wanna see Santa," then Jill sneezed and blew her nose into a linen hanky.

That sneeze at this stage of the disease could spread the causative virus—Varicella Zoster.

"I don't know if it's the chickenpox making her sneeze or that fireplace. The chimney sweep popped in yesterday and said there was no reason to worry about a chimney fire yet. He was booked solid, but he'd come and sweep it as soon as he could."

"I wanna see Santa," the child repeated.

Mrs. Driscoll tousled her daughter's hair. "I know, pet. Let's hear what Doctor Laverty has to say." She looked at Barry with pleading in her eyes.

"I'd like to have a look at you, Jill."

"I'll help you, pet. Sit up and raise your arms."

She obeyed and Mrs. Driscoll hauled the child's white nightie over her head. "There now." She set the nightie aside.

Barry had no difficulty recognising the crops of unilocular little sacs, some filled with turbid fluid or pus, others which had ruptured and were turning or already had turned into silvery scabs. They were mostly scattered on her chest, back, face, and arms. He nodded to himself. No doubt about the diagnosis, but until every vesicle had dried up into a scab, and the virus was no longer in the nasal mucus, the patient must be quarantined. No point beating about the bush.

He squatted. "Mrs. Driscoll. Jill. It is chickenpox. I have no treatment but the soothing lotion you're already using. At least some scabs are forming, which means it's nearly over—"

"Then can I go to Belfast to see Santa?" Jill was excited.

Barry glanced up, looked at Mrs. Driscoll, and gave a practically imperceptible shake of his head. "I'm sorry, Jill," he said, "but I can't let you out until the blisters have stopped forming and every last one has scabbed over."

Her little face crumpled, and the tears came.

Barry stood to let Mrs. Driscoll get Jill back into her nightie and hug her daughter. "I'm sorry too, but even if you can't go to see Santa," she nodded her head toward the fireplace, which let another wisp into the room, "you can still send a letter to him at the North Pole on Christmas Eve."

Jill sighed, leaning her head into Mrs. Driscoll's breast. "S'pose so. I want a dolly's pram and," her shoulders heaved, "I want to go back home. I miss my daddy." She sobbed and made a wailing sound.

Mrs. Driscoll tightened her hug and stroked her daughter's hair.

Barry's heart ached for the little girl. He waited for several minutes until she had calmed down before saying, "Mrs. Driscoll, I'll need to wash my hands. I can't risk spreading the infection."

"Of course. Bathroom's two doors on your left. There's a clean towel on the wall rack opposite the sink."

"Thank you."

When he returned, he found Mrs. Driscoll waiting in the hall holding his coat. "She's nodded off."

"I'll not disturb her then."

She helped him on with his overcoat.

"I don't mean to pry, but she's very upset about not being at home with her father." Eighteen months ago, he'd not have brought the subject up, but he'd learnt from O'Reilly that it was a doctor's job to care for the whole family.

She shook her head. "We had a row. I blew up, waited until Declan had gone to his work the next day, packed a few things, and brought Jill here to this cottage."

Barry frowned. "Why here?"

"The cottage has been in our family for years. It came down to me from Granny Buckley. She died a year ago. Of the lupus. That's why I was so terrified when I saw the rash on wee Jill's little face. I hoped to heaven it was chickenpox, but I couldn't sleep last night from the worrying and this morning I just had to know. Thank you for coming, Doctor. You've set my mind at ease, so."

Mrs. Driscoll looked around the room. "I'd wanted to come here to see the place again ever since Granny died. When the tenants moved out a month ago, I knew I had to come. But Declan wouldn't. Too busy with his work. And his road bowling."

"I see."

Barry knew he was moving onto thin ice but said, "It sounds like Jill wants to go home."

She frowned. Pursed her lips. Looked down.

Barry waited.

"He'd promised to take me out for dinner. I had the babysitter in the house. But he and his stupid road bowling friends had won some trophy that afternoon and he came home scuttered at midnight." She looked into Barry's eyes. "It wasn't the first time, but it was the last straw. I couldn't stay. It took us two days to get here by bus. If he'd just agreed to come here with me. Make time for Jilly and me. I still love him, but I'll not make the first move, so."

"I see." This was one proud and stubborn woman. And hurt. An idea was germinating, but for now Barry decided to let the hare sit. "I see. I hope he will."

"Me too." She sighed. "I'll just have to bide and see. But right now my main priority is Jill. She's missing her Da and wants to see Santa. I can't promise she'll see Declan, the *omadán*—" She must have seen Barry's puzzled look. "Sorry, Doctor, the idiot, but I can do my best to see she gets to meet Santa." She nodded her head toward the room where Jill was sleeping.

"I'm sorry I've spoiled her trip tomorrow, but she should be over being contagious soon. It usually takes four to five days for the blisters to scab up. Once every last one has, your daughter will no longer be infectious."

"And do you know where there might be another place I could find a Santa for her?"

Barry smiled. Now he truly could help. Fingal took great delight in his annual role. "The Ballybucklebo Bonnaughts Sports Club's party is next Wednesday afternoon. Santa will be there. That's five days from now."

"That's perfect," she said, her eyes bright. "But are you sure? It sounds like a private club."

"It is, but Doctor O'Reilly's on the executive. I'll talk to him.

I can't make any promises she'll be all right by then, but I'll pop in on Wednesday morning and if she's all clear, Jill and you will be able to go."

"Honest to God?"

Barry nodded.

"I pray to God my Jill will be able to go to the party." She smiled. "I'll just have to keep my fingers crossed, but that would be the best Christmas present for my wee girl."

Next to having her daddy back, Barry thought but said nothing.

The surgery had run late so Fingal O'Reilly was finishing up his lunch of vegetable soup and Kinky's leftover apple crumble with toffee sauce. He was taking his last spoonful when Barry came in. "Busy morning?"

Barry sat in his usual place. "Not too bad. But two more cases of chickenpox."

"The sooner we have a decent vaccine for it the better."

"I agree. I want to ask you about one—"

Kinky appeared. "Welcome home, Doctor Laverty. Here you are." She set a steaming bowl of soup in front of him.

"You'll enjoy that, Barry," O'Reilly said.

"It smells delicious. But, Kinky, before I start, I need some help."

She smiled. "Whatever I can do."

"I remember you telling me you've an older brother, Tiernan, who was a keen road bowler."

"He still is, the goat. They're all mad for the road bowling in Cork."

O'Reilly heard the deep affection in her voice.

"I need to get in touch with a man called Declan Driscoll. He's a bowler too. From Bandon."

"I'll see what I can do on the telephone, so, but don't let your soup get cold." She left and Barry took a spoonful.

O'Reilly asked, "What were you going to say?"

"Right. One of the kiddies with chickenpox is new here. Could we invite her and her Mum to the Sports Club's party?"

"Of course, if the kiddie's not contagious and—"

The front doorbell rang. Kinky would answer it and if it were a patient, Barry would handle things. For the first time in six months, Doctor Fingal Flahertie O'Reilly had no need to worry about it. He settled back in his chair and enjoyed the luxury of having help again.

Kinky appeared. "It does be his lordship, so."

O'Reilly sat bolt upright as John MacNeill entered. "Fingal. Barry. No. Please don't get up. Fingal, I need your help."

"Of course."

"The ground staff have pulled a wildcat strike at Heathrow. Andrew got stuck in London. He's been at an airport hotel. The ferries are booked solid, but I've been able to pull strings through old service connections and got him a Transport Command flight from RAF Brize Norton to RAF Aldergrove this afternoon arriving at two."

"Well, that's a fine way to be welcomed back to your home after thirty-five years away."

The marquis nodded his agreement. "Isn't it just. He sounded pretty done up. I'm thinking now I should have met him in London, but Myrna talked me out of it. Said he was bound to be tough after all those years in Australia and he could look after himself. But he sounded so frail on the phone when we talked this morning. I was driving through Ballybucklebo and I suddenly thought,

I'd like a doctor present. I know it's abominably rude of me to just show up here, but could you possibly come to Aldergrove with me, Fingal?"

"I can." O'Reilly said. "I'll get my coat and bag."

4

There Is No Place like Home

O'Reilly and John MacNeill sat in the heated comfort of John's 1960 Bentley S2. The grey gloom of the afternoon drizzle was punctuated by dozens of blinding lights at ground level. O'Reilly watched spellbound as a uniformed aircraftman slowly helped a civilian down the stairway from the transport aircraft onto the tarmac of RAF Aldergrove.

They were followed by troops being ferried home to Ulster for the Christmas holidays.

"That's him, Fingal. It's Andrew. I-I must say, I'm rather nervous. I haven't seen the man in more than thirty-five years. He may be my brother, but he'll be like a stranger."

"He's your flesh and blood, John. That bond is strong."

"Yes, I dare say you're right. Thanks, old friend." John MacNeill put a hand out to grasp O'Reilly's shoulder, as if for support, then wordlessly the two climbed out just as Andrew and his escort came to a halt at the car.

"Colonel Lord John MacNeill?" the aircraftman said.

"Yes."

"May I help your brother into the car, sir? He's a bit shaken up. We hit some turbulence."

"Please." John held the back door open, his gaze following his brother into the car, then watched as the young serviceman gently helped Andrew MacNeill into the backseat, covering him with a tartan rug and arranging pillows at his back.

O'Reilly heard a muffled "Thank you very much," from the backseat.

"I'll be back with Mister MacNeill's luggage, sir."

John climbed in beside his brother, O'Reilly took his place in the front passenger seat, and together they closed the doors against the cold.

The two men shook hands.

For a while no one spoke. With a great roaring of rotors and a stink of aviation petrol, a helicopter had taken off making speech impossible. The noise increased as the huge craft passed overhead, then gradually faded.

"Andrew. Welcome home. Welcome home. It's been a very long time."

O'Reilly could hear a softness and warmth in John's normally steady tones.

"John. Good to see you too. Very good." Andrew had to pause for breath and gulp in a lungful of air. "It's been a long journey. I'm whacked, and the last leg in that airborne cattle lorry? It defies description. Iron seats, cold, crammed in like sardines, thrown about like clothes in a tumble-dryer. Perfectly horrid. Bloody strike."

His tones had an edge and the man was trembling, whether from the cold or from anger O'Reilly could not be sure.

"But you're here now," John said, "with your family, and that's all that matters. It's only half an hour to Ballybucklebo House and it's warm and comfortable there."

"So, I'm almost home. God, it's been so long, John. So very long."

This time O'Reilly heard a distinct catch in the man's voice.

"And the sooner I get you there the better. I've brought my friend Doctor Fingal O'Reilly. I'd like him to take a quick look at you. You said in your call that you were ill. I want him to make certain we can go straight home, and you don't need to go to hospital. So, I'm getting out and he'll get in here. Fingal, I won't drive off until you're finished."

O'Reilly and John changed places. The car shook as the boot was opened, luggage loaded, and the lid closed.

"How do you do, Mister MacNeill?"

"How do you do, Doctor? And it's Andrew."

Hands were shaken.

"Thank you." O'Reilly turned to his patient and began taking his pulse. "Now on a professional note, can you tell me what your doctors have said is wrong with you?"

"They told me it was leukaemia two weeks ago."

O'Reilly flinched. In 1936, his own father had contracted leukaemia—a rapidly progressive type of the disease—and had died six weeks after his son's graduation ceremony. That was twenty-nine years ago, and the sadness was still there, but this was not the time for personal matters. Andrew MacNeill needed O'Reilly's undivided attention.

"I'm sorry, John," said Andrew on hearing his brother's sudden drawing of breath. "I didn't want to say anything until I knew I was here, safely. It's bad, I know."

Like any layman, John would instantly assume that leukaemia was a short-term death sentence. O'Reilly resumed taking Andrew's pulse. It was 110 per minute. Fast but not surprisingly so given the emotional circumstances. O'Reilly put the back of his hand on Andrew's forehead. No sweating and it was cool so no fever. "Did they say if it was acute or chronic?"

"All I heard at my last appointment was that I'd a few months left, tops." Deep breath. "I'm afraid I didn't wait around for the particulars. That's when I decided I wanted to come home for the last time."

"And I'm delighted you did, Andrew," John said in a low voice from the front seat. "The priority now is to establish, with Fingal's help, exactly how you are and what can be done. Get you back home and into bed. You sound exhausted. There'll be plenty of time for catching up later."

"I've missed you, John. And you're right, I am done in." A pause for breath. "You always were my friend. Stood up for me."

"You were and you still are my younger brother. I'm sorry I haven't been able to do more."

O'Reilly saw Andrew frown and a glistening at the corner of the man's eyes but knew he had to continue with his questions. "Did your doctor say there was anything else?"

"Yes. At my first visit he told me I'm anaemic. I'm taking iron for it."

"I see." O'Reilly took out his pocket torch and shone it onto Andrew's right eye. "Look up." O'Reilly pulled down the lower eyelid. The inside of the lid beneath the conjunctiva, the transparent membrane that covers the eyelids and the eyeball, allows an observer to see the state of the blood vessels beneath. In this case they were pale. Anaemia all right. He turned off the light and released the lid. "And how do you feel right now?"

"Short of breath, dog-tired, and trying to put that wretched flight in the past."

"You are still anaemic, that's why you're breathless. It's one effect of having leukaemia and so is tiredness, never mind the added travel fatigue. Just let me take your blood pressure."

It was down a tad, but no cause for concern. Vital signs would remain pretty stable in cases of leukaemia until shortly before the end. "Andrew, we don't need to take you to the hospital tonight. John, I'm coming through to the front seat so you, Andrew, can stretch out here and try to get some sleep. When we get you tucked up at home, I'll take a proper look at you. Try to give you both a clearer idea of what I think is going on."

"That," said John MacNeill, "would be very much appreciated, Fingal."

The moment O'Reilly was seated up front John MacNeill engaged the gears and began the journey to Ballybucklebo House. Only a few more minutes to put an end to an almost four-decade absence for Andrew MacNeill.

O'Reilly stood and watched as Lord John MacNeill, with the proficiency of a trained nurse, assisted his brother, now in red-and-white-striped pyjamas, into a four-poster bed, covered him with the bedclothes, and propped him up on pillows.

There was a knock on the door.

John called, "Come."

A maid in a white cap, black dress, and white apron, dropped a small curtsey and said, "Cook sent up a pot of tea, sir. She thought Mister Andrew might like a cup after his long journey." She set a tray on the bedside table.

"Thank you, Bess." She withdrew.

John stuffed two more pillows behind Andrew's back and lowered him onto them. "All right?"

"Yes, thank you." His voice was weak.

As John worked, O'Reilly studied Andrew's features. He had the MacNeill nose, unlike the marquis was clean-shaven, and his hair was dark not iron-grey. But there was no question about them being brothers, although Andrew had the deep tan of a man who had spent much of his life in the hot dry climate of Western Australia.

John walked round the bed. "Milk and two sugar as I recall?" He poured and gave the cup to Andrew, who sipped.

"Lifesaver," he said. "Thanks. And you did remember."

"Good. Now I'm going to leave you alone with your doctor. If you need anything—either of you, just ring and," he pointed to a long bell-pull hanging by the top right-hand corner of the bed, "Bess will be up at once." He started to walk toward the door, "Please come and talk to me, Fingal, after you've finished."

O'Reilly heard the door close behind him. He set his bag on the floor and sat on the edge of the bed. "So, Andrew, I know you are very tired."

"I am, Doctor." He yawned and covered his mouth with one hand. "It's a bloody long way from 'the great south land.'"

O'Reilly could detect an Australian overlay to Andrew MacNeill's upper-class English tones, notable by the lengthening of his a's.

"I'll try to keep this short so you can get a decent sleep."

"Thank you." He took another long swallow of his tea.

"How long have you been sick?"

"I went to a specialist in Perth about six months ago when I started feeling pretty crook."

"In what way?"

"Tired. Bruised easily."

"I see." That was nonspecific. Could be quite a few things.

"He did some blood tests. Told me I was anaemic, and my platelets were a bit low, white cells were down a bit, and probably taking iron would help. Last thing he said was, 'No worries, mate. She'll be right.' I was reassured, I can tell you." He inhaled. "I'm not sure the iron did much good, and I'd read that older men can bruise easily for no good reason. It was still happening and I was still tired, but I was able to get most of my work done at the mine, so I didn't think about it too much. Decided to tough it out. See him in six months as he'd suggested."

"I see." Interesting. So, a diagnosis of leukaemia had been made only two weeks ago. Six months ago, it hadn't even been hinted at. Had O'Reilly's Antipodean colleague not actually made the diagnosis of a rapidly lethal condition back then? Initially, in the acute leukaemias, anaemia, low platelets, and paradoxically also the white cells were low in the early stages. The leukocyte levels would rise dramatically as the disease progressed. Had his Australian colleague simply made a mistake because the initial blood work was unusual? Doctors did make mistakes.

"Two weeks ago, I went back to Doctor Kelly for my checkup. Told him I still had the same symptoms. He took lots more blood, sampled my bone marrow—and that hurts like blazes, I can tell you. Then all long-faced, he told me I wasn't long for this earth. Few months tops. Leukaemia." Andrew sighed. "That's a bit hard to hear when you're only sixty-two."

"It must be. You have my sympathy."

O'Reilly looked at his patient and knew the next question was a crucial one. He always tried not to ask leading questions, but this was important. "Have you had any bleeding from your mouth? Nose?"

Andrew blanched. "No. No, not at all." He set his cup and saucer on the bedside table.

Good, O'Reilly thought, because it was an almost invariable accompaniment to advanced acute leukaemia. He'd try the question he'd asked at Aldergrove one more time. "Did your doctor tell you if the leukaemia was acute or chronic?"

"You asked me that before and, Doctor, I can honestly say I don't remember. All I took in was that I had a few months left. Suddenly, the only thing I wanted to do was see John, see Ireland again. Pay my respects to this place. First, though, I'm afraid I stayed full as a goog for a few days."

O'Reilly "A what?"

"Full as an egg—drunk." He grimaced. "Probably not prescribed for my condition. Once I'd sobered up, I thought it over for a while, wrote a very long letter to my lawyer, phoned John, packed some bags, and got on a bloody aeroplane."

"I can certainly understand that." The poor divil must be scared skinny, but he was doing a good job of hiding his concerns. "I'd probably have done the same, but it may not be as bad as that. Let's have a look at you."

"Yes, please carry on, Doctor."

When O'Reilly finished, he had observed that the liver and spleen were both enlarged, the spleen not enormously so and that was a good sign. He had been able to palpate enlarged lymph nodes in the neck and armpits. Andrew's pulse was still a little fast, not unusual in an anaemic patient, and there were no signs of fever. O'Reilly straightened up and stuck his stethoscope back into his jacket pocket.

"Well, Doctor?"

O'Reilly looked the man in the eye. "I'll not beat about the bush. You do have signs of leukaemia."

"Blast." He shook his head. "I just kept hoping it might go away, or that the doctor in Perth was wrong. But deep down, I knew things weren't right." He began pleating the sheet between his fingers, focusing on the task as if it were of vital importance. He didn't look up.

"But, and it's a big but, I don't know which kind."

Andrew frowned, looked up. "I thought there was only one kind and if you had it, you'd soon be, as my foreman at the mine might say, 'dead as a drowned dingo.'"

O'Reilly had to stifle a smile. "Actually, we recognise six types and I'll not bore you with the details, but the six are divided into three acute and three chronic—and the outlook differs considerably depending on the specific type." O'Reilly did not want to give false hope, but he was reasonably sure Andrew MacNeill's disorder was chronic, not acute as Father's had been.

"So, I've still got a fighting chance?"

"I don't make promises unless I know I can keep them."

"I understand."

"I'll need to seek specialist advice."

"At Christmas?" Andrew's face collapsed. "In the season to be jolly? Ho, ho, ho, and all that? Bloody hell."

The man's façade was starting to crack. O'Reilly put his arm round Andrew's shoulder. "I can understand your disappointment, your anger at having to deal with the uncertainty. But there is hope. And I will do everything I can to help. That is a solid promise."

"Thanks, Doctor." He turned, punched one of the pillows to rearrange it, and lay back. "I appreciate that, I do. Now . . ." He pulled the bedclothes up to his chin. "I think I'd like a little shut-eye."

"I understand." O'Reilly rose and as he picked up his bag and walked to the door to turn out the lights, he was sure he could hear gentle crying.

John MacNeill was putting two pieces of turf on the fire when O'Reilly walked into the study.

John straightened, putting the poker back in its place. "I'm very anxious to hear what you have to say, Fingal, but please have a seat. Let me get you a drink. The usual?"

"Please."

John went to a six-legged Sheraton sideboard to pour a small Jameson Irish whiskey into a Waterford cut-glass tumbler. O'Reilly sat in an armchair in front of the fire. He noticed in one corner of the room an undecorated, seven-foot-tall fir tree standing in a two-foot wooden box and held upright by a series of wooden braces. He and Kitty would have to get their tree soon. John always let Fingal cut one on the estate.

"Here you are, Fingal."

"Thank you. Myrna not home?"

"My sister has a late end-of-term meeting at the university this evening."

Myrna Ferguson was a doctor of science in Queen's, a degree that took academic precedence over a PhD, and a full-time senior faculty member in the chemistry department.

"I'm not disappointed that she's not here. Andrew and I were close. I'm afraid he and Myrna were not. She blamed him for so much that happened in our lives around that time." John sighed as he sat and raised his glass to O'Reilly. "I won't trouble you with those details. Cheers," he said, and O'Reilly replied to the toast and took a restorative swallow of his own drink.

"So, what can you tell me about Andrew's condition?"

"All right," he said, "I am fairly sure Andrew has a leukaemia."

John frowned and, sitting very stiff-backed, said, "A leukaemia?"

"Yes, as I told him, there are several kinds of the disorder in two distinct groups, acute and chronic. I'm almost certain his is not acute and that's good because those are the bad ones."

John's frown deepened. "I'm not sure I understand. You think my brother's isn't acute. May I ask why you think that?"

"Because patients with the acute ones often bleed as the condition worsens. Andrew has not, and they are much, much more common in childhood. Your brother is hardly a child." O'Reilly drank some more of his whiskey.

John managed a small smile. "I'm no spring chicken either," he said thoughtfully. "Now that he's back, it's as if no time has passed at all. All I can think about is us living in this house as small boys. We were so close." He took a sip of his drink. "So, there's hope, Fingal? Truly?"

"I can't promise anything, but yes, there is some hope." Now he had to tell the unvarnished truth. "In all honesty, I can't give you any certainty of a good prognosis, but there really is a chance. It'll take some blood work, possibly a marrow biopsy, and an expert opinion to be sure."

"It'll be tricky getting one at this time of the year."

"True and, again, I don't want to hold out false hopes, but I think young Doctor Laverty might be able to assist us. Not over the weekend, but I'll ask him first thing on Monday."

John frowned. "So, you do think Andrew's got a real chance, Fingal?"

O'Reilly produced a small smile. "Your brother's very tired and when I looked under his conjunctiva at the airport, I could tell that he's anaemic. If it is chronic lymphatic leukaemia, the long-term outlook's relatively good. And if he's given a blood transfusion, he'll certainly feel very much better, have much more energy. Earlier, we discussed taking him to the club's Christmas party. Despite how he is tonight, we might still be able to get him there."

John smiled. "He'd like that, I know."

O'Reilly finished his whiskey. He rose. "Now, unless there's more I can do for you, John? If you'd not mind, I'd better get home. For the time being Andrew needs lots of rest and plenty of good grub, which I'm sure Cook will be only too happy to make for him. I can't do much more medically, but if you're worried . . ."

"Thanks for everything you've done already, Fingal. Having something to hope for is very comforting." John rose. "I'll ring for Thompson to drive you home and I'll go up to check on Andrew."

"Thanks, and I'll pop in on Sunday just to see how he's doing."

"That would be much appreciated." John set his drink on a table. "And if you'd like, why not bring Kitty? Stay for lunch."

"That's always pleasant. I'm on call, but Kinky can always reach me here. I'm sure Kitty will be delighted."

John smiled. "We always enjoy your company. And, actually, it might not hurt to have guests. Myrna can have a very rough edge to her tongue, but if you're here, it might encourage her to mind her p's and q's."

If it wasn't enough for John MacNeill to be worried sick about his brother's health, he had to play peacemaker in long-standing family politics. And at Christmas too.

5

I Have Hope to Live

O'Reilly swung the long-nosed Rover right, through a gap in the traffic on the Bangor to Belfast Road. He drove past a red-brick gatehouse that stood guard over two high wrought-iron gates, each bearing the crest of the marquis, and onto the upwardly winding drive to Ballybucklebo House. As promised on Friday, O'Reilly was making a home visit today.

Gravel crunched under the car's tyres, and a weak sun cast misshapen shadows of evergreen trees onto the lawn. Some years ago, they had been exemplars of the topiarist's art. Today, O'Reilly had difficulty determining whether one was meant to be a horse, a rabbit, or a ruptured duck. Lord John MacNeill had been hit hard by death duties when his father had died in 1951, and the new marquis had been forced to make economies.

"Look out, Fingal," Kitty yelled as one of the estate's hand-reared cock pheasants, with red cheeks, dark green head, and the white neck ring which gave him his name—Mongolian ring-necked pheasant—strolled nonchalantly in front of the car.

"Phew," Kitty said. "I know you take a cavalier attitude to cyclists, Fingal, but I shudder to think what might have happened if you'd hit one of John MacNeill's birds."

O'Reilly drove on. "He would not have been pleased and we might have lost our invitation to his traditional New Year's Day shoot. Thanks for the warning."

"My pleasure, old bear."

"Here we are," he said as he parked outside the "big house" with scarlet-berried cotoneaster clinging to its Georgian front wall.

"Hop out." As Kitty did, he collected his bag from the back-seat.

The front door opened and Thompson, the marquis's butler/valet, came to attention.

O'Reilly gave Kitty his arm and together they climbed the broad flight of three steps.

"Good morning, Commander and Mrs. O'Reilly. May I wish you the compliments of the season?"

"Morning, Thompson." O'Reilly had been a Surgeon Commander and Thompson a gunnery Chief Petty Officer on the battleship HMS *Warspite* during the war. "And a merry Christmas to you too."

"His Lordship is expecting you, sir. He and his sister Lady Myrna are in the study. Please follow me."

Thompson led them to the dark wood-panelled room where Lord John MacNeill sat in an overstuffed armchair gazing at an oil painting of him and his late wife, Laura. O'Reilly estimated the work had been painted in 1950. There was a red setter in the painting; its successor Finn MacCool lay at his lordship's feet. Myrna looked up from her book, set it aside, and smiled at the visitors from where she sat in a second armchair, one of five arranged in a semicircle in front of the fire. The scent of burning peat filled the room.

John MacNeill rose, made a little bow to Kitty, and offered Fingal a hand, which was duly shaken. "Fingal, Kitty, grand to see you. Kitty, please have a seat." He indicated one near Myrna who smiled and patted its cushion. John said, "Fingal,

I do appreciate your coming to see Andrew again. He's still upstairs."

"In general, how is he?"

"Weak, short of breath, but not quite so tired. He slept from after you left until four yesterday. Today he's been dozing on and off. I've hated to wake him."

"I'm not surprised. It's more than a twenty-four-hour flight from Australia and his body thinks it's eight at night. If that's not enough, as Andrew described it, the RAF transport plane trip must have been gruelling for him too."

John glanced at his sister and smiled. "A friend of mine took him up in a two-seater when he was seventeen. He's hated flying ever since. I think it shows a certain strength of character to submit himself to something he feared because he was so keen to see Ulster and his family again."

"Pity our brother didn't show that strength of character in the twenties." Myrna scowled. "There you were following the family tradition in exemplary fashion, joining the Irish Guards. And I was starting my doctorate of sciences—"

"No mean feat," said John, "for a woman in the Roaring Twenties and the thirties. Did you know, Kitty, that Myrna was the first—"

"I was not boasting, John, and please don't try to change the subject. I was commenting on our brother. Father always believed if you wanted something badly enough it was up to you to work for it. That boy had every possible advantage of class, education, and money and what did he ever achieve before he went overseas?" She made a strangled noise in her throat. "Mother was never the same after Andrew left. I believe he broke her heart."

"Myrna." John's voice held a note of warning, as if this were an argument of long-standing.

"I don't care, John. Fingal and Kitty are our friends. I'll not put on a social façade for them." She paused. "I'm not a great believer, but perhaps this illness is some kind of divine retribution."

Kitty bridled. "Myrna Ferguson, he's your brother, he's sick, and it's nearly Christmas Day. Please."

Myrna stared at the fire.

O'Reilly was surprised by Myrna's vehemence, and by Kitty's words. Still, on more than one occasion, O'Reilly had heard Myrna say she valued Kitty's frankness. The two women had not known each other long, but they had quickly developed a friendship. He wondered if this were the best time to leave the room. But Kitty had reached over and lightly touched Myrna's shoulder and the older woman had reached out to grasp Kitty's hand. As usual, his wife seemed to have things in hand.

"I'll just nip up and take a quick peek at him. I can find my own way." He left and walked along a hall decorated with portraits in oils of previous marquises. As he climbed a broad staircase, the patterned carpet held in place with shining brass stair-rods, he remembered John's words of last Wednesday about Myrna and Andrew. "She had very little empathy for him then. I hope she will have more now." From her last remark it seemed she hadn't changed.

He came to the bedroom door and knocked.

"Come."

O'Reilly let himself in. The daylight came in past open heavy maroon curtains.

Andrew was still in bed, sitting up, and reading a copy of the *Sunday Times*. "Good morning, Doctor." He folded the paper and sat up with an effort. "There's an interesting article in here about the Russian Mikhail Sholokhov." Deep breath. "He's just won the Nobel for literature."

If Andrew could be interested in the news, he must be feeling better. O'Reilly hitched his backside onto the side of the bed and took Andrew's pulse. "Interesting. I enjoyed *And Quiet Flows the Don*." He smiled. "But I'm here to ask how you are?"

"A bit better rested. Still very short of breath. Tired, but you know John, he thinks a shave and a haircut are the universal cure-alls and after today I'm inclined to agree with him. He had your local barber," he paused to take another deep breath, "come by yesterday evening. That Dougie George is something." Andrew smiled. "He told me Australians had been invented so Americans would appear to be cultured."

O'Reilly laughed. "Insulting people is Dougie's stock in trade. He's known locally as our belligerent barber."

"I think he did a good job, don't you?" Andrew turned his head from side to side.

"Yes indeed." Today, in the light of day, O'Reilly could see an echo of the dashing young rake he must have been in the 1920s.

"If I'm going to the Sports Club . . ."

"And I hope you are. We'll know by tomorrow. Your pulse is normal today and—" O'Reilly held the back of his hand to Andrew's forehead. Cool and dry. "And you've no fever." There wasn't much more to look for until they could get some blood test results.

"Good. I'm not in the bush now. For the sake of the family, I must keep up appearances." He inhaled. "Something I neglected to do some years ago."

O'Reilly was curious but waited to hear what the man might say.

"I'm not sure John knows what to do with me. Faultlessly solicitous about my health, but we haven't talked about much else. And being here again brings back all the old memories."

The man was breathing heavily and O'Reilly wondered how he might keep him calm, but it seemed Andrew O'Neill was bent on confession.

"I was young, just out of a boys-only boarding school when I started to go off the rails." He gulped for air. "Fell in with a bad lot. Champagne is quite exhilarating, you know, and girls?" He inhaled deeply and it probably wasn't just because of his anaemia. "You don't mind me telling you this, Doctor? You know I'm not sure how long I've got left. I don't have a priest to confess to." He smiled. "The MacNeills are not Catholics."

"It's safe with me."

"Went to Cambridge. John was rarely home when I came home for hols, but we kept up a wonderful correspondence. At first Father treated me like a spoilt kid, but when I was home after Trinity term for the summer, he was not impressed when he had to bail me out of the cells in Bangor late one night. Drunk and disorderly.

"My sins finally caught up with me when I got myself in deep debt gambling. Terrified of facing the old man again. Thought I could recoup my losses, so I had a couple of wealthy club members each cash a cheque for me. I simply wrote them at the bar and accepted the cash. I bet the lot on a horse—that lost. Naturally when my friends tried to lodge the cheques, they bounced. I'm afraid that sort of thing just wasn't done at White's." He looked up at O'Reilly and inhaled deeply.

So that explained the mystery of the White's expulsion.

"Finally, he packed me off to Australia. John applied for compassionate leave so he could see me off, but he was in India and was denied. But Myrna?" He shook his head, his breath laboured. "We'd never been close, even as children."

"Have you talked since you came home?"

"Briefly. She's very distant." He picked up the newspaper, then dropped it.

"Don't know what the hell got into me back then. Perhaps I thought John was better than me, though he never behaved like that. Sure, I was tired of the rigid discipline at Harrow and found little or none at Cambridge, but . . ." He fell silent and bowed his head. "Just a silly young man?"

O'Reilly nodded. "Does it matter now? Regret is probably the least useful of the emotions."

Andrew's smile was wry. Self-deprecating. "I stayed in touch with a friend from Cambridge. It was he who let me know the Sports Club was raising money for their renovations. Father's monthly remittance wasn't ungenerous and Australia had hit me like a pail of cold water to the face. I worked, saved my money, and eventually bought what was thought to be a tapped-out gold mine. Best gamble I ever made."

"John's told me about the money you gave the club."

"Yes, trying to atone, I suppose."

Neither man spoke for a minute or two. Andrew had closed his eyes and O'Reilly wondered if he'd fallen asleep, but suddenly he opened them and sat up straighter.

"I'm not going to hide in my room." He stretched out an arm. "If you would give me a hand, Doctor." He gasped in a deep shuddering breath.

O'Reilly reckoned it wasn't just the anaemia. Andrew MacNeill was hurting inside.

"I'd like to wash my face, put on my dressing gown, and come down for lunch."

"Please forgive my state of undress, everyone. I think it would be too tiring struggling into my clothes," Andrew said. "Doctor O'Reilly has been of great assistance to me."

John MacNeill instantly put down his drink and was on his feet, put his arm round his brother's shoulder, and helped him to an empty armchair next to Kitty. "How are you feeling?"

"Thanks, John. Tired, but happy to be home."

"And we're all glad to have you home. Allow me to introduce Mrs. Kitty O'Reilly? Kitty, my younger brother, Andrew. Home from Australia."

"Pleased to meet you," Kitty said.

Andrew managed to hold himself more erectly. "And you. May I call you Kitty?"

"Of course."

"Kitty, Fingal is a very skillful and understanding physician."

O'Reilly, now sitting beside Myrna, watched as Andrew MacNeill discretely but unmistakably surveyed Kitty from head to toe. What had he just said about his misspent youth? It had all started with champagne and girls. And here was this sixty-two-year-old man, possibly on death's door, flirting with his wife?

"I had no idea you had such an attractive wife, Doctor." He took Kitty's hand and raised it to an inch from his lips before releasing it. "You must be the star of the County Down."

"You're too kind, Andrew." Kitty smiled, clearly pleased by the compliment but said, "And did you know at one time Fingal played rugby football for his country and was light-heavyweight boxing champion of the Royal Navy's combined Atlantic and Mediterranean Fleets?"

Andrew's laugh was hearty until he was forced to take a deep breath. "Fortunately, I'm in no shape to try to contest you, Fingal, but forty years ago—"

Myrna spoke. "Forty years ago, if any woman wore a skirt, she was fair game to you, Casanova."

"I see you're as gracious as always, sister. Not very complimentary to our guests to suggest I'm as undiscerning as that." Andrew smiled at Kitty.

"Myrna." John was still standing. "I don't think, particularly as Andrew is so ill, that was very polite." And in an obvious endeavor to let matters cool down, he asked, "Fingal, the usual?" and started toward the sideboard.

O'Reilly ordinarily would simply have nodded but to keep the mood neutral he said, "Please, John. Small Jameson, and, Andrew, I'd advise you to have a soft drink. Alcohol will hit you very hard in your present condition."

Myrna's retort was swift and venomous. "His present condition? Huh. It always did, Doctor. My middle brother had no self-control. None whatsoever." She stared past Fingal. "Our father, Victorian gentleman that he was, had little time for the weaker sex apart from our mother. Much preferred his sons—"

And is that, O'Reilly thought, what had driven this strong-willed woman to excel as a scientist, a profession, with one or two notable exceptions, that was essentially closed to women?

He was aware of Andrew saying in a low hurt voice, "Well, perhaps I won't be here much longer for you to disapprove of, sister."

Myrna's hand flew to her mouth. She sprang to her feet. "I'm sorry everybody. Oh, Andrew," and with that she fled.

6

Examine Well Your Blood

"Morning, Barry," O'Reilly welcomed his young colleague into the dining room at Number One Main at eight thirty on a drizzly Monday morning. "Cuppa?"

"Please. It's miserable out there." Barry sat as O'Reilly poured.

"How was your weekend?"

Barry smiled. "Mum was like a dog with two tails. Spoiled me rotten. Mum and Dad are sorry they can't make it to your at-home on Christmas Day. They're going to other friends in Donaghadee, but Sue and I will be there if that's all right?"

"Course it is."

"Thank you."

Kinky had come in to clear away a plate bearing the wreckage of a brace of kippers. "Archie and I will be pleased to see to the catering. And it will be grand to see your Miss Nolan again, Doctor."

"Yes, it will," said O'Reilly, raising an eyebrow in Barry's direction and watching the young fellow blush. His hand went instinctively to his fair tuft to smooth it.

Kinky handed O'Reilly a sheet of paper. "Your list, sir."

O'Reilly accepted the list of patients who had requested home visits today. "Thanks, Kinky," he said to her departing back but did not hand it to Barry, who frowned. "Change of plans, Barry. I need your help."

Barry's cup stopped halfway to his lips. "Oh?"

"Yesterday I saw Lord MacNeill's brother from Australia." He paused and as O'Reilly had anticipated, Barry did not interrupt to ask questions. "He has been told he has leukaemia, but I can't tell if it's acute or chronic. I need specialist help to determine which. I do know he's clinically anaemic. I know John is very keen that Andrew attend the Sports Club Christmas party on Wednesday if at all possible. I'm sure it would mean a lot to both brothers if we could get him well enough to go."

"So, you're hoping it's chronic and that he can have a blood transfusion to correct his anaemia and give him more energy, right?"

O'Reilly nodded. "But I need to short-circuit the system. We haven't time to refer him to Doctor Nelson's clinic at the Royal. You have a friend, don't you, who's a pathologist?"

"Harry Sloan. He's in his second year of training." Barry smiled. "You'd like Harry to see your patient, test his blood at once, and make a diagnosis? Let me make a phone call."

Barry vanished. O'Reilly helped himself to a second piece of toast and another cup of tea. Barry Laverty was very quick on the uptake, and in medicine, as in all things in Ulster, it really wasn't so much what you knew as who you knew. He buttered his toast and spread some Frank Cooper's Oxford Marmalade, the one commercial preserve Kinky would permit in the house.

Barry was back before O'Reilly had finished eating. The young man was smiling. "I got through to Harry. He wants you to get the patient directly to his office in the Clinical Sciences Building. He'll take the samples himself, prepare slides, and examine them. If he's not certain about what he's seeing, he'll ask Doctor Ingrid Allen, a senior pathologist, to take a look—she has a particular interest in haematology. It'll only take her a few minutes to look at the slides. And if your patient has a chronic form and a transfusion is needed, Harry'll have a plan ready to use the normal admission system for it."

"Wonderful, Barry. Now I need another favour. I seem to have been saying that a lot lately. I can't imagine how I've managed without you these past six months."

"Ah, Fingal," Barry said. "You've grown accustomed to my face."

"Professor Higgins. *My Fair Lady*." O'Reilly laughed and started to hand the home visit list to Barry who, even before he accepted it, said, "I know. I'll take the surgery and do the home visits after lunch because you're going to drive the patient to the Royal Victoria Hospital."

"Mind reader." O'Reilly left his tea and toast and rose. "I'll just phone the MacNeills so Andrew's ready when I get there."

O'Reilly headed for the hall, lifted the telephone receiver, and dialled. "Hello, Thompson."

O'Reilly left John MacNeill helping Andrew up the front steps and into the Royal Victoria's Clinical Sciences Building not far from the hospital gates on the Grosvenor Road while he parked his car and returned. "Here I am."

John had found a chair for his brother.

"Not far to go now. If you could bring Andrew to the lift, John?" He pushed the call button and inhaled the predominant smell, a mélange of floor polish, tissue preservative, and animal scents from the vivarium.

The bell chimed and the three men entered. "Floor three, Barry told me," O'Reilly said.

The lift ascended and stopped, and they left to be confronted by a sign over the door, DEPARTMENT OF PATHOLOGY. NO ADMITTANCE.

"Hang on." O'Reilly stepped into a room where three secretaries were typing. "Excuse me."

"Yes."

"I'm looking for Doctor Sloan."

A small bespectacled woman began to frown. "You're not supposed to be in here."

"I'm Doctor O'Reilly from Ballybucklebo. We've arranged to see him."

She smiled. "That's all right then. Harry's down the hall. Third door on the left."

"Thank you."

He returned. "Nearly there."

John glanced back at the NO ADMITTANCE sign. "I don't think the public is supposed to be in here, Fingal, and I don't wish to intrude. Would you like me to wait in the cafeteria? I know you'll explain it all to me anyway."

"I think not, sir." Here in the hospital, it was proper to afford Lord MacNeill his due. "We're dealing with a serious condition. I'd like you to stay in case your brother needs more support than I can give."

"Fair enough. I'll stay."

"Thanks, John," Andrew said.

John let Andrew lean on him and together they made slow progress along a linoleum-covered floor to the third door on the left. It was open and inside a seated, white-haired young man was peering into a monocular microscope.

"Doctor Sloan?"

He swung in his chair. "Doctor O'Reilly? Mister MacNeill, and—?"

"Lord John MacNeill."

Harry was on his feet at once. He bowed his head. "My Lord."

"Please be seated, and 'sir' is just fine, young man. Please try to pretend I'm not here. I came to support my brother."

"Thank you, sir. Thank you." He glanced round the office. "Have my seat, sir. I'll only be a minute." Harry vanished.

John pulled a chair out from under a shelf and helped Andrew sit.

Harry returned carrying a chair and accompanied by a laboratory technician bringing in a stool.

John MacNeill took the chair. O'Reilly perched on the stool.

Harry turned to O'Reilly. "And how's my old classmate, Barry? He told me he's come back to work with you—for good."

"He's fine. Sends his regards and, yes, I'm glad to have him back."

Harry Sloan turned to Andrew. "I'm sorry for your troubles, sir. Seeing you for my friend Barry is the least I can do. Please consider it an early Christmas present."

Andrew managed a weak laugh. "I'll reserve judgment until I get my results."

"Fair enough. I have everything ready, so if you'd take off your overcoat?"

Minutes later, Harry Sloan was drawing the necessary samples, and O'Reilly was looking curiously round the office, noting two walls covered in floor-to-ceiling bookcases filled with learned tomes and atlases of colour photos of tissue samples. One of the books caught his eye, *Boyd's Pathology,* which looked to be more than a thousand pages. He wondered how anyone could spend so much time writing it. Didn't pathologists miss working with live patients? He certainly would.

"All done." Harry put a wad of cotton wool over the withdrawal site and taped it in place. "Now, if you'll excuse me, I'll go and make the slides and examine them." He collected a number of full rubber-corked glass tubes. "If you'd like coffee?"

O'Reilly nodded.

Andrew said, "I'd prefer a tinnie of Swan Lager, but yes please."

Harry laughed and left the room.

John helped Andrew back into his coat, and the younger man busied himself adjusting his clothing and trying to get comfortable. He ended up sitting nearly upright, not unlike his older brother's military bearing. But O'Reilly knew Andrew MacNeill to be a tired man and, despite his attempted humour, a worried one.

"Excuse me." The bespectacled woman who had earlier been typing carried a tray in and set it on the shelf. "Your coffee and some digestive biscuits, gentlemen."

"Thank you," O'Reilly said.

They helped themselves.

"He's gentle, is your Doctor Sloan," Andrew said.

"Barry says he's an excellent pathologist too."

"And we very much appreciate your attention, Fingal," John said.

O'Reilly shrugged. "We all at the Sports Club are very much indebted to you, Andrew, for your gift back in '51, even though we didn't know it until now."

"Even after all these years in Australia, I've never lost my affection for County Down and Ballybucklebo. And when an old friend from Cambridge sent me a newspaper clipping in 1951 about the club needing money, it seemed the right thing to do."

John said, "You may have left Ulster under a cloud, brother, but your stock is very high with the Bonnaughts' executive."

O'Reilly approved of John's no doubt deliberate avoidance of mentioning the party. That was sub judice until today's test results were in.

John said, "Andrew, I still don't know much more of your doings since 1926. You've spent the better part of Saturday and Sunday sleeping or dozing."

John's a clever man, O'Reilly thought, getting his brother talking to keep his mind off what his results might show.

"Well," said Andrew, glancing over at O'Reilly, "I'll bet my existence came as something of a shock. I've had quite a life Down Under—so far . . ."

O'Reilly detected anxiety in Andrew's voice.

"But I've not heard much about what's been going on with the family here either."

John said, "I'm afraid the MacNeills haven't been very lucky. I was married. I have a son, Sean. He's a captain in my old regiment, and your nephew."

"I hope I'll get to meet him."

"So do I, because the family's getting thin on the ground." A shadow passed across John MacNeill's face. "I lost my wife Laura in 1955."

Andrew put a hand on his brother's arm. "I suspected something of the kind, but I didn't know. I'm so sorry."

"I-I don't like talking about it."

"Of course."

"I know the few encounters you've had with Myrna have already been thorny. She's had her share of misery too. Her husband died in a hunting accident in '59. They had no children."

"Good God. I knew she was some kind of professor at Queen's. Just assumed she was unmarried." Andrew took a deep breath. "Lord, but I run out of puff so easily. I'd no idea, but it's my own fault. You tried to reach me, John, several times I know, but . . ." He screwed his eyes shut, shook his head. "I was ashamed of why I was in Australia, and I wasn't too proud of what I was doing there other than making money."

O'Reilly waited.

Andrew opened his eyes. "Let me put it this way. You said the MacNeill family is getting thin on the ground. Not in Western Australia. You've a nephew of thirty-three with two kids of his own and a niece of twenty-nine who shares her aunt's penchant for higher education and is still unmarried. And they're all called MacNeill. Not that they've any idea they're twigs of a noble family."

"Good Lord," John said.

He inhaled. "And there may be one or two more I'm not sure of."

"Out of wedlock?"

"Fraid so, and I wasn't very good at 'in wedlock' either. I'm three times divorced."

John stretched out his hand and touched his brother's arm. "Andrew, in all honesty I cannot say I approve—"

"Deep down I didn't either. That's why I couldn't reply to your letters. Just couldn't see myself confessing it all."

"Well, as far as I'm concerned, Andrew, I am completely willing to put it behind us. And while I will understand perfectly if you wish to return to Australia, if you decide to stay in Ulster, I will make you welcome, brother."

"Thank you, John. Thank you."

O'Reilly sat quietly, not wishing to intrude. He was curious to learn more, but Harry Sloan appeared.

His face was calm. "It's chronic lymphatic leukaemia." He took his seat. "We're certain."

So, the doctor in Perth had been mistaken. Well, none of us are infallible.

Andrew looked at O'Reilly for an explanation. "Andrew, under the circumstances that's the exact news we've been hoping for."

"Actually," said John with no hint of facetiousness or self-righteousness, "I've been praying for it."

Harry Sloan looked directly at Andrew. "I had Doctor Allen confirm the diagnosis. Eighty-five percent of the abnormal white cells are small lymphocytes. We don't even need to do a marrow biopsy."

"Honestly? Honestly? I don't know what those kinds of cells mean, but I know you're telling me I'm not going to die in a few months." He screwed up his face.

O'Reilly put a hand on the man's shoulder. He was shaking. "Honestly, Andrew. It is true." This was not the time to go into the fact that many patients with chronic leukaemia lived for five to ten years. This was a time to celebrate today's reprieve and, as O'Reilly was fond of remarking, cross the other bridges when they came to them. He glanced at Harry for confirmation.

Harry continued, "It's still a serious condition, of course, but at the moment you don't even need treatment, although it's available if and when it becomes necessary. Except for the anaemia—that's always present in patients with this kind of leukaemia. Your haemaglobin is low and you do need an immediate blood transfusion. But we have matters in hand there too. I've identified your blood group. O positive, the commonest type and two pints are being cross-matched for you as we speak. By the time you've completed the routine admission procedure and are in a bed, they'll be ready."

"Dear God," Andrew said. "Doctor Sloan, you said I was to consider this an early Christmas present. It's the best one I've ever had in my life. Thank you, Doctor."

"Us pathologists don't get thanked by patients very often . . ."

Andrew smiled. "Well, you're getting thanked by this one. Thank you, Doctor Sloan. Thank you."

"All you have to do, sir, Doctor O'Reilly, is wait for the wheelchair I've sent for and trundle Mister MacNeill round to admitting. It's well signposted on the main corridor. And after the transfusion, Mister MacNeill, you'll be amazed at how much better you're going to feel."

"It's true, Andrew." O'Reilly turned to John MacNeill, "I know you two have been hoping to come to the Christmas party. I'm pretty sure you will be. I can't promise you a tinnie of Swan Lager, but there'll be mulled wine."

All four men gave release-of-tension laughs and Harry Sloan said, "I'll send you a copy of the results, Doctor O'Reilly, so Mister MacNeill can show them to any other doctor he might see in the future."

"Thank you," O'Reilly said, "and here's the chair."

A porter parked it in the hall and left.

John helped Andrew to his feet and gave his brother a hug. "Thanks a million, Doctor Sloan."

7

These Things in a Green Tree

Barry was sitting in the upstairs lounge in front of the fireplace, gnawing on the end of a yellow pencil and staring at the *Times* folded on his knee. Fourteen across, nine letters: "Unorthodox messenger endlessly carrying quote about." He was stumped, and he even had a couple of letters. He heard O'Reilly saying, "Go in there, Arthur. Get yourself warm."

Arthur Guinness was so-called because he was Irish, black, and had a good head, just like the stout. Barry looked up to see the big Labrador tumble into the room, barely acknowledge its occupant, and go straight to the front of the roaring fire.

O'Reilly came in. "Lie down, sir."

Arthur flopped on the rug and was given a dirty look by Lady Macbeth, but the animals' Christmas truce seemed to be holding.

Barry shifted his attention from the puzzle. "Well? How did it go at the Royal?"

"Well. Very well. Chronic lymphatic, heaven be praised."

"Wonderful news, Fingal. At least in the short term." Barry smiled. "I'm sure everyone's relieved."

O'Reilly nodded and headed for the sideboard. "Andrew's not overjoyed about having leukaemia, but he understands that if he must have it, he's got the least of the evils. Your friend Harry Sloan worked wonders and I've just dropped a less tense and much brighter Andrew MacNeill and John back at Ballybucklebo House, and now my tongue's hanging out. Would you like something?"

"No, thanks. I'm still on call. I'll be having one with my meal. I'm expected for dinner at Sue's flat in Holywood at six."

"Fair enough." O'Reilly poured himself a Jameson. "How was your day?"

"Pretty gentle. Small surgery and only one home visit. Another little girl with chickenpox."

O'Reilly planted himself on an armchair beside Barry. "That's country folks for you. Unless it's urgent, or like chickenpox and affects the kiddies, they realise we need less work too at this time of the year." He sipped his drink. "Probably out doing their Christmas shopping. Done yours?"

"I have."

"Good. Me too." O'Reilly hunched forward, his glass held in both hands. "Thanks for the favour."

Barry shrugged. "We've always worked like that."

"Good man, and let's keep on doing it. Except for some naval exceptions on old *Warspite,* I've never been one for rigid routine."

"Which is more than can be said for the maypole apparently. I ran into Cissie Sloan this morning. You know Cissie. Never happier than when she's gossiping about something. Seems they were hauling up the traditional star on a halyard arrangement, usual routine that they've been doing for years, and it got stuck. Halfway up. They sent a council workman up in a bosun's chair, and he got stuck. It took all of the Bangor fire brigade to get him down."

O'Reilly laughed. "Never a dull moment here in Ballybucklebo. Did they eventually get the star up?"

"Dunno, but I'll see on my way to Holywood."

"Anyway, I'll see for myself. I'm going to nip over to the Duck, and tomorrow, if you don't mind, I need the morning off."

"So, you'd like me to take the surgery?"

"Please. Kitty has a few days' leave and she's going down to Dublin to visit her mum. Staying overnight but she'll be back on Wednesday in time for the Sports Club's party. We'd like to get our tree before she goes. Take that great lummox," he nodded to a snoring Arthur, "for a really long walk. He missed his today."

Barry smiled. "Why not? I'll let Mum know not to expect me until lunchtime."

"Bless you, my boy. Kitty will be delighted. I'll do the home visits in the afternoon and the after-hours emergencies and Wednesday's surgery."

"Fine by me, and Kinky or someone here can answer the phone and reach me at Sue's this evening."

"Grand," said O'Reilly. "Grand altogether. That'll work and there's something else I have to tell you about. We're under contract to provide twenty-four cover, but it doesn't necessarily have to be provided by us. There's an organization called the Contactors Bureau. It was set up by a Doctor Barry Bramwell. Young trainee doctors can sign on for twelve-hour shifts. GPs can hire the service so if one of their patients calls, the staff of the bureau gets the call and contacts the young doctor by phone or walkie-talkie. The GP pays a fee to the bureau, to be divided between them and the young doctor."

Barry knitted his brows and nodded. "Sounds like it could give us both a break now and then."

O'Reilly drank more deeply. "They'll cover us from noon,

Wednesday the twenty-second, so we can go to the club's Christmas party, and continue to cover us until nine A.M. on Boxing Day. It's a Sunday so the surgery will be closed then anyway. I'll take call, and you can have another day off."

"Thank you. I like the sound of that." He smiled. "So will Mum and Dad. And Sue."

"I'm sure they will."

Barry rose. "I've got to go. Sue will give me bread and water for dinner if I'm late there." He dropped the *Times* on the table beside his chair. "If you'd like a bit of a brain teaser, take a look at this. I'm stumped by fourteen across. I'd been staring at it for five minutes before you came in. But only that one clue, mind."

O'Reilly leaned over and peered at the puzzle. "Hmm. Okay. I'll give it a go. Have fun and give her our regards."

"Will do."

Barry started down the stairs, and by the time he got to the landing, O'Reilly had bellowed, "Heretical." Barry rolled his eyes and smiled. Ten seconds. That had to be a new record for his senior partner. Barry heard the sounds of Bing Crosby's velvet tones. O'Reilly had switched on the wireless and was humming along to "It's Beginning to Look a Lot Like Christmas."

He remembered his friend Jack Mills, now a surgeon in training, remarking some years ago, "Bloody silly song that. Toys in every store? Why on earth would an ironmonger's or a greengrocer's stock toys?"

Barry went into the kitchen. Kinky was roasting something for dinner and it smelled mouth-wateringly good. "Have a good evening, Doctor Laverty." She turned from where she was stirring a mahogany-coloured, fruit-studded Christmas pudding mixture in a large ceramic bowl.

"Thanks, Kinky. That certainly looks delicious."

She smiled. "Just like Ma down in County Cork taught me when I was a girl, so. I do make them the year before. This is ready to be put into individual bowls and stored in my pantry. I'll pour a little brandy over them from time to time until next Christmas. This year's will be perfectly ready on the twenty-fifth."

"I'm sorry I'll not be here."

"Go on with you, sir. I'm sure your mother's a fine cook."

"Very, but there's only one Kinky Kincaid when it comes to the kitchen."

Kinky coloured and Barry could see she was pleased as she stirred the mixture with greater vigour.

He opened the fridge and took out a chilled bottle of Entre-Deux-Mers. "Thanks for chilling it for me."

"My pleasure. And there's a little something for Miss Nolan's tree, so. They do be my gingerbread men, perfect size for ornaments." She pointed to a small bakery box tied in jute twine.

"Thank you, Kinky. Sue will be thrilled, and I'll bet they'll be as good to eat as they are to look at." He showed her a slip of paper with Sue's telephone number. "You can get me here if someone needs me."

"Please leave it on the counter, sir. And mind you don't eat that gingerbread until after Christmas."

Barry was stopped by Ballybucklebo's lone traffic light. He looked up to see an illuminated golden star on the very top of the maypole. Strings of fairy lights ran from beneath the star at acute angles to the ground. So, by hook or by crook and almost certainly with help from the fire brigade's extension ladder, persistence had won the day.

The traffic light changed, and he drove along Main Street, where shop windows on both sides were lit up, some with festoons of fairy lights, others with spray-on white frost. Dougie George, Ballybucklebo's bellicose barber, had dressed his window with a scene in which Santa, brandishing a huge pair of scissors, seemed to be giving a shaggy Rudolph the red-nosed reindeer a haircut.

Farther along, the lawn outside the Catholic chapel was decorated with an illuminated Nativity scene with shepherds and sheep, wise men with camels, Mary and Joseph and baby Jesus in the manger.

As he headed for Holywood he started singing, off-key of course, "It's beginning to look a lot like Christmas. Tiddley tiddley pom." Perhaps it wasn't such a daft song after all.

Once Max, Sue's springer spaniel, had executed his usual ritual of barking uncontrollably, putting his front paws on Barry's crotch, completely ignoring Barry's yells of "Gerroff," and finally submitting to being hauled away by Sue and made to sit, Barry could safely greet her with a hug and a kiss. "Kinky sent a box of her gingerbread men for the tree and her love—and I've brought you mine and a bottle." He kissed her again.

"Kinky is such a darling." Then she took his arm and led him into her front room.

"I'll go and pop this wine in the fridge."

"I've a better idea. Let's open it, pour a couple of glasses, and then pop it in the fridge."

"Good. Let's."

In the kitchen, where saucepans bubbled on the stove-top, it took Barry little time to remove the cork and pour. Lifting his glass and looking into their astonishing greenness, he said, "Here's to your bright eyes." They took his breath away as he sipped his wine.

"Come on, love," Sue said, "back to the sitting room. And you," she pointed at Max who was trying to follow, "my sweet but silly dog, you must stay here, or we'll never get the tree decorated."

Sue closed the door behind her, leaving Max to whine and then fall silent.

"Oh, Barry, I'm so glad you could come over tonight and I hope you don't get called away. I've a distinctly non-Yuletide dinner planned, fillet steak, roast potatoes, and boiled carrots." She sipped her wine, and Barry his, then they set the glasses on a low table in front of the sofa. "Now let's get the tree seen to."

"Sure." As he passed the lit electric fireplace, Barry noticed several Christmas cards on the mantelpiece. One caught his eye. It read on the front, HAVE A COOL YULE. "May I open this?" He'd always been taught it was bad form to read other's personal messages without permission.

"Of course," Sue said from where she was opening a box of Christmas decorations. "It's from one of my cousins in Philadelphia."

Barry opened the card and burst out laughing. "'And later, man—like wow!'" What on earth it meant he had no idea, but he chose to make his own interpretation. He cocked his head and grinned at her. "I could fancy a bit of like wow! with a certain copper-haired school mistress."

Sue laughed. "You, Doctor Laverty are incorrigible. Down boy. We've a tree to decorate. Come on."

He gave a vast mock-sigh, returned the card, and joined her where she knelt beside an open box of decorations and a five-foot fir tree, its wooden, supporting base wrapped in scarlet crepe paper.

She handed him a shiny red glass sphere with a loop of golden twine for attaching it. "Here, we'll do the balls first starting at the bottom. I've got red and green ones, so alternate them please."

"Yes, Sergeant. To hear is to obey." He put down his wine and saluted.

"Eejit." She blew him a kiss.

Barry started hanging them from the tips of the lowest branches and gradually working upward. "Decorating trees always takes me way back to decorating with Mum while Dad was at sea during the war." He smiled. "It must have been hard for her, having him away, never knowing where he was, how he was. But somehow she always made Christmas magical for me." He bent and kissed her. "And now you do."

Sue shook her head and smiled. "I love you, Barry Laverty, and it must have been difficult for her. I was lucky. Farmers weren't called up. Someone had to feed the nation. Christmas for me was always with Mummy and Daddy."

"You were lucky. And it still was magical for me, as it should be for all children." And suddenly he thought of little Jill Driscoll.

Sue laughed. "You're right, and the tree is all part of it—and on this one, little animals come next," she said, and handed him a pink horse.

They worked together, Sue handing, Barry hanging.

Barry paused from positioning one of Kinky's exquisite little gingerbread men, then stood back to look. "It's coming on a treat." He sighed. "Not everyone is happy this time of year. I saw a case on Friday I can't stop thinking about."

"Oh?"

He hung another ornament. "A little girl who isn't having much fun. She's got chickenpox."

"Och, such misery, and at Christmas. Poor little mite."

"She missed seeing Santa in Belfast on Saturday. I'm going to call on them Wednesday morning. I hope she'll be well enough to see Fingal playing the Sports Club's Santa that afternoon."

"Me too, Barry. So many of the kids at MacNeill Elementary were off school with it before we broke up for the holidays."

"If having chickenpox and missing Santa wasn't bad enough, this little girl's mummy and daddy separated a few weeks ago, and she wants them to reunite."

"Heavens. I'm hardly the font of all gossip in the area, but I don't think I know any families that have separated. Who's the mother? Do I know her?"

"You might. The wee girl's six so she'd have to have been going to school, I think. Her name's Jill Driscoll from Bandon, County Cork."

Sue nodded. "Jill Driscoll. Sure, I remember her. I met her three weeks ago when her mother brought her along to register for school. It's a statutory requirement for newcomers. She's to start in January. Her mum's Finella, right?"

"That's right. She's a pretty young woman with shoulder-length auburn hair—"

"Is she now? I hope that's a professional observation, not a social one."

Barry heard the suggestion of an edge in Sue's voice.

"Don't be daft." He warbled, off-key as usual, a few lines of "I Only Have Eyes for You."

"But I am intrigued by her story. Single mother, at least temporarily, living all alone but for her daughter, far from home."

Barry finished hanging the decoration. "Come on, let's get our tree finished."

Sue handed him a little unicorn. "From Cork, you said? Well, if I know Kinky, that young woman will not be alone for long. You know how Kinky loves to mother waifs and strays."

They worked steadily together.

"I told Kinky about Jill and Finella on Friday. Mrs. Driscoll and her husband fell out over something to do with road bowling. Kinky's already phoned her brother, Tiernan, who's a bowler, and he's trying to contact Declan Driscoll."

Barry wrapped a golden wire six times around the tree's leader to fix an angel with a long white robe and golden wings atop a tree festooned with glass balls, little animals, tinsel, gingerbread men, cotton wool for snow, and a string of many-coloured fairy lights. "All done."

He stepped back, put a hand on each hip, and said, "A thing of beauty—just like my girl." He turned around and kissed her, then he pointed to the socket in the skirting board where the lights' flex was plugged in. "Why don't you do the honours."

Sue bent and flipped the switch down.

And among the green needles, little conical lights shone green, red, blue, and yellow.

Sue straightened up and Barry joined her. He put his arm around her waist.

She leaned against him and put her head on his shoulder. "It is pretty, isn't it? Makes me feel like a little girl again too."

Barry nodded. Felt a nostalgic lump in his throat.

"I do hope everything does work out for your patient and her mother," Sue said.

"Me too."

They stood together in silence until Sue said, "I've got some other decorations, holly and a twig of mistletoe to put up, but dinner will be ready soon. Let's bring our glasses through to the kitchen. The table's already set in there. We'll have dinner then finish decorating the rest of the living room."

"Sounds good to me," Barry said and crossed his fingers hoping he'd not be called away before they hung the mistletoe.

8

On a Tree by a River

"Morning, Barry," said O'Reilly, glancing up from the remains of his poached eggs on toast. He thought Barry looked well rested. "How was your second night? Getting used to your old attic room?"

"Morning, Fingal. Kitty." Barry took his place beside O'Reilly at the top of the table and smiled at Kitty who was sitting opposite. "My room is as comfy as ever. Like coming home." He helped himself to a bowl of cornflakes and added milk. "I'm sure one of Kinky's breakfasts will be streets ahead of hospital kitchen grub, and my evening was lovely, my night unbroken."

Kinky appeared and removed O'Reilly's and Kitty's plates. "Good morning, Doctor Laverty. I hope you slept well."

"I did, thanks, Kinky, and that hot-water bottle was much appreciated."

"This old house was built long before that new-fangled central heating and I can't have you catching cold just before Christmas. Now, how would you like your eggs and how many?"

"Just one please. Lightly poached."

Kinky tutted. "Only one, is it? You'll waste away, so. I don't know what young people see in those dried cereals. Not fit for a cow to eat, if you ask me. Are you sure I can't give you two? Freshly laid, yesterday? Nice brown ones?"

Barry laughed. "All right. Two it is."

O'Reilly saw her pleased smile. Kinky Kincaid was at her happiest mothering somebody. Archie Auchinleck was a lucky man. O'Reilly and Kitty rose as Kinky left. "Barry," he said, "I've asked you for two favours in two days, now I need one more."

Barry helped himself to a cup of coffee. "Go ahead."

"There was a call last night, just about the time you and Sue would have been sitting down to your meal. Colin Brown's mum thought he was developing chickenpox. Wanted to know if he should be confined to quarters. Hell, they live near the Mucky Duck, so I nipped over. Took a look. She's right."

Barry said, "So you took my call for me? Thank you."

"Didn't take long. Today I'm running Kitty up to Belfast to catch the Dublin train after we've finished on the Ballybucklebo Estate—"

"So, you'd like me to pop in and see Colin after surgery before I head home?" Barry shook his head. "Of course, I will."

"Thanks."

"Dear old bear," Kitty interrupted. "That's what I call him." She smiled at O'Reilly. "You've a heart of corn."

O'Reilly shrugged and looked down as he always did when embarrassed by a compliment. "Didn't someone write about there being 'no blessed leisure for love'?"

"Thomas Hood, wasn't it?"

O'Reilly grinned. "I just thought you should have some leisure, that's all."

Barry laughed. "Off the pair of you go to walk old Arthur, get that tree, and enjoy your morning. Your leisure. And Kitty, have a pleasant visit with your mum in Tallaght."

"Thank you, Barry. I will."

"And you, Doctor Laverty," said Kinky, bearing a fragrant plate, "enjoy your breakfast. I put on a couple of rashers. Johnny Jordan, the butcher, sells very good ones, to keep the eggs company. A young man like you needs to keep up his strength, so. And you can take your time. The waiting room's half empty." She smiled. "I think you're going to enjoy this morning's surgery. Most of the patients are holding parcels wrapped in Christmas paper. It's going to be crowded under that tree, so. Get a fine, tall one, Doctor dear."

Arthur Guinness couldn't control his throaty mutterings as the Rover ran up the driveway to Ballybucklebo House.

"John's not expecting us to call in. He knows we're off to Belfast. I'm sure Andrew will be feeling much more lively since his comforting news and his transfusion."

Once past the house, the car bounced over a rutted track across a field leading to the Bucklebo River, which flowed through the estate. "I'm going to park at a spot where Barry likes to fish, and we can walk to the spruce grove."

The car passed under some leafless ancient elms. Branches scraped the windows until, leaving the small wood behind, they entered a broad meadow. The lane crossed the field heading toward the banks of the river where equally bare weeping willows grew in a meandering pattern along the river's bends. Their branches swaying in a light breeze shed a coating of hoarfrost that tinkled to the ground.

When the lane petered out, O'Reilly parked. Sunlight dappled the water's wavelets flowing from left to right. The shallow edges were trimmed with jagged fingers of sparkling ice as if they were decorating the river for Christmas.

O'Reilly, warm in his Paddy hat, heavy sweater, Barbour waterproof coat, and corduroy trousers, heard his boots crunch as he got out and let Arthur out of the back.

"Sit."

The big Lab obeyed.

O'Reilly reached in and brought out a large hacksaw, perhaps not what a specialist would have used, but it always had done the trick on Christmases before. He closed the door. "Heel."

Arthur tucked in, his breath coming in steaming puffs, and followed as O'Reilly walked to the front of the car where Kitty, also warmly clad, waited. His gloved hand took hers. "Nippy but crisp," he said as they strode off. "There's a Norwegian spruce grove about three-quarters of a mile ahead. One of John's predecessors imported and began planting the trees in the mid-nineteenth century after Queen Victoria and Prince Albert made them popular at Christmas. The grove's renewed on a regular basis and is opened to the locals on the Saturday before Christmas Day so they can come and for a small fee cut a tree. It used to be free, but the estate has to pay for itself now."

Kitty stopped and took a deep breath. "What a lovely tradition." She looked around and took another deep draught. "Smell this air. It is good to be with you, here in Ballybucklebo, Fingal. I wasn't sure I wanted to leave Belfast. I mean, I knew I wanted to be with you."

"I hope so," he said with a small smile.

"I just wasn't sure about leaving the city. I've almost always lived in cities, except for those years in Tenerife during the '30s. I knew nothing about rural life here." She reached down and picked up a tiny branch that had fallen off a tree. "I do love it in Ballybucklebo, and I love you, my old bear." She lifted the branch to her nose. "What a wonderful smell. We were told in one of our nursing courses back in Dublin that Norwegian spruce beer was once used as a cure for scurvy."

O'Reilly laughed. "Kinky makes sure we get enough citrus fruit, so I'll stick to Guinness if you don't mind."

"Eejit." And Kitty began swinging her hand, forcing him to comply, and they continued along like a couple of lighthearted kids enjoying the day.

They fell into a companionable silence and walked past a still, deep pool shaded by a willow and farther upstream alongside a long ripple that flowed from the downstream tail of a wide bend in the river.

The only sounds were the cawing of a parliament of rooks overhead, the occasional bleat from a flock of black-faced ewes on the opposite bank, the crunch of their boots on frost, and Arthur's panting.

"All right," O'Reilly said as they passed through a meadow dotted with clumps of yellow-flowered gorse, their almond scent discernable on the slight breeze. "Arthur. Hey on out, boy. Hey on out."

Arthur, nose to the ground hunting for scents, big otter tail upright, black coat glistening, quartered the ground. He froze, raised his head, stared ahead, and charged, to O'Reilly's surprise, not toward the nearest clump of gorse but farther along the river. Up sprang a ball of teal clawing for height and making frantic kekking cries. The little ducks were uniformly drab because when the hens started laying earlier in the year the cocks moulted into dowdy eclipse plumage.

"Come in, boy."

The big dog obeyed and sat in front of O'Reilly. Arthur's nostrils let go puffs of condensation. He slowly shook his head as if to say, *Sometimes I don't know why I bother. I thought you were meant to shoot one or two so I could retrieve them. I like retrieving.*

O'Reilly let go of Kitty's hand, transferred the saw to his left hand, and picked up a stick from the riverbank. "All right. I'm sorry, but I'm not going to shoot any of those ducks, Arthur, but here's the next best thing." He hurled the stick ahead. "Hi lost."

Off Arthur ran, and by the time he had made several happy retrieves, O'Reilly said to Kitty, "Here we are."

The spruce grove, its perfume scenting the chilly air, was studded with sap-oozing stumps where the villagers had taken their share of Christmas trees. "Still plenty left to choose from." O'Reilly told Arthur to lie down. "How about this one?" he said, eying a tall, bushy specimen.

"It's beautiful. It almost seems a shame to cut it down." Kitty walked around the tree and reached out to touch one of the branches. "But you don't think it's too tall for our lounge?"

O'Reilly looked the tree up and down. "Nonsense. It's perfect."

"But you're more than six feet, and it's towering over you."

"The lounge has nice high ceilings. Fine Georgian houses always do. I like a good-sized tree. And I'm going to fell it well up from the ground. Not uproot it."

"I think it's too tall."

"But not too wide. It's beautifully proportioned. The perfect Christmas tree."

"I agree. It's a lovely shape. It will fit into the corner very nicely. But I still think it's too tall, Fingal."

O'Reilly looked around. No other tree seemed to have the shape and presence of this one.

"What about that one?" Kitty said, pointing to a much smaller tree. "That's a lovely size."

"That scrawny thing. Wouldn't give it house room. This is the one."

Kitty laughed and the sound seemed to echo around the grove, blending in with the sighing of the wind, the bickering of the rooks. "Yes, this is the one, Fingal."

He set to, low on the trunk, the teeth of the saw rasping on the bark. "It's one of my earliest memories of Christmas when we were living in Holywood before Father moved the family to Dublin. He used to take my brother, Lars, and me into the Holywood Hills on Christmas Eve to cut our tree. We'd decorate it that night, put the presents under it. Then we were allowed to open one present, hang up our stockings on the mantel, and leave some eggnog for Santa and a carrot for one of his reindeer." He swallowed. "I'll always remember my feelings of happy awe the first time I was old enough to understand and came down on Christmas morning to find the nog drunk, the carrot gone, sooty footprints on the hearth, and our stockings filled."

Kitty said, "I can just picture you as a little boy, Fingal, so full of wonder. It really is a magical time for a child." He heard a little catch in her voice. "I wish we'd had some."

He stopped sawing, and holding the tree with one hand, stood up. "Do you mind?" He paused and swallowed. "Mind very much?"

"Sometimes." Then she smiled. "But then I remember how lucky we are to have found each other again. We have each other and we can enjoy other people's children tomorrow at the party."

"That," said O'Reilly, "is true on both counts, my darling." He began to saw again.

"You'll make a magnificent Santa. Kinky said she was going to Alice's this afternoon, so she's happy to pick up your Santa suit."

"Good. I'm afraid she had to let out the waistband—again." He felt the tree start to move away. "Kitty, could you hold the top, steady it on the side opposite me? I'm nearly finished, and I want to make it a clean cut."

"Right."

One more long stroke.

"That's her," O'Reilly said. "Let me take it, if you'd carry the saw." He set the saw on the ground, pulled some coils of thin rope out of a coat pocket, and began to wrap the tree, feeling the needles tickle his face. "Now, let's get our tree home and you to Belfast. Heel, Arthur." And off they set, carrying the ancient green symbol of Christmas, and bearing with it, for O'Reilly, all the fond memories of Christmases past.

With the tree propped up in the corner of the upstairs lounge, its leader well below the ceiling, Kitty safely seen off on the train, and Barry by now at his folks' place in Ballyholme, O'Reilly sat by the fire with Lady Macbeth on his lap and Arthur snoring contentedly at his feet. The breeze had a knife edge to it now, and O'Reilly had brought the old dog into the house. The feelings of nostalgia, which had been started when the tree was cut, had lingered. Praise be, there had been no requests for home visits and no emergency calls.

Kinky was busy in her kitchen making sausage stuffing, and chestnut stuffing, one of each to be put into the turkey's two open ends.

Before he'd come upstairs, he'd opened the one locked

drawer in the roll-top desk in the surgery. He'd already read several of his old letters to Kitty since she'd given him the bundle. Today's frost had made him think of another frosty night this year. Tonight would be the first time since their marriage that O'Reilly would be alone in their bed, and he felt like reliving, through his letters, a part of their second courtship.

He opened the envelope, noted the date, January 16, 1965, and began reading.

Dear Kitty,

I'm writing this letter after seeing you off back to Belfast following our dinner. I had wanted to tell you how much being with you means to me, but, as usual, couldn't find the words to say so when you were here.

Before you arrived, I had been sitting in the lounge dipping into William Butler Yeats's The Winding Stair and Other Poems. *I was trying to concentrate, but the knowledge that in minutes the woman with whom I've been in love all my life would be in this house kept interrupting, but doing so joyously. You bring your brilliance and warmth into this old place where I've lived since 1946, alone but for my books, my music, my dogs, and recently a kitten. But the house has had no woman's touch but Kinky's mothering one.*

Rereading "In Memory of Eva Gore-Booth and Con Markiewicz"—"Two girls in silk kimonos, both Beautiful, one a gazelle"—made me think of my gazelle, my Kitty, coming for our weekly dinner, the highlight of my week. Regular phone calls are good, but they're not the same as having you near. It is wonderful to me how easily we have eased into our old, happy, comfortable ways together, just like in the thirties, before I let you slip away.

When Kinky answered the front door, the thought of your presence made me tingle. I rose and poured the chilled sauvignon blanc I have come to learn that you enjoy.

You came in grinning from ear to ear. I love your face when you smile, but then I love you no matter what you are doing. "Welcome." I handed you your wine.

You bent, kissed me. "Hello, old bear. Have you missed me?"

"Lots," I'd said, "but you have your work in Belfast, and even with Barry's help, I still have to be here."

O'Reilly leant back from his reading, glad he had felt compelled to record the small details of their time together. But why, he wondered now, as he had then, why didn't you propose? You knew you loved her. Had done since you met her in Sir Patrick Dun's Hospital back in the thirties. Loyalty to your late wife Deirdre's memory? Reticence? Fear of rejection? He chuckled. It didn't matter, because he had done so not long after that night and she'd accepted.

He read on.

You sipped the wine and went and sat on the sofa.

I admired the neatness of your figure in your suit, the curve of your calves, the easy swing of your hips, but I have always been hesitant to compliment a woman, even one so very near and dear to me, on her physical attributes. I suppose I am a bit of a throwback from Queen Victoria's day. Father was a Victorian and passed on to both Lars and me how he believed a gentleman should act toward ladies.

I caught a faint suspicion of your Je Reviens and to me

the perfume said, "Kitty." It still lingers and tells me, like a siren's song, to be with you forever.

When you walk into a room, I am a young man in his twenties, besotted with the young nurse with grey amber-flecked eyes.

I sat beside you. You were pleased as punch that one of your staff nurses had been promoted to junior sister. I admire your concern for your staff and how you have always cared for your patients.

When I kissed you, your lips were soft, warm. And inwardly, although excited, I berated myself for letting you and your kisses slip away for so long.

Your breathing was more rapid when you pulled back and went to top up our glasses.

On the way back, you stopped by the stereo, selected a gramophone record, and popped it on. I recognised the work. Miles Davis, Reflection.

You came back, handed me my glass, and sat.

I have come to know you don't like it if I talk when you are listening to music, so I simply held your hand, sipped my wine, and savoured watching how your expression kept changing as the moods of the passages changed. I favour the classics, some modern pop like the Beatles, traditional jazz. You favour modern jazz, which I have some trouble understanding. That's perfectly all right. We don't have to like all the same things.

I could tell you were lost in the sounds, carried on the waves of emotion that were echoed in the expressions flitting across your face—a smile, a frown, a wrinkling of your nose. A line from Shakespeare came to me. "If music be the food of love, play on."

There was a sad, slow passage and I watched silver tears leak from under your lids and I used my thumb to dry them. You opened your eyes and gazed into mine. I bent to you and our lips met, gently, caressingly, moist and warm.

In that moment I needed no more. For two people as much in love as us, love is in a glance, a kiss, in being held and warmed and comforted, being halved when apart.

I saw your smile, and said then, as I am writing now, Kitty O'Hallorhan, I love you, darling . . . now and forever.

Fingal

O'Reilly sat back in his chair, slipped the paper into the envelope, and stroked a purring Lady Macbeth. Enjoy your time with your mum, Kitty, my love, and come home to me soon. He moved the little cat aside, went to the record rack and put a disc on the turntable, then sat again to be washed by Miles Davis's *Reflection,* letting the musical notes take him back to that evening, just as the tree had become his time-machine to Christmases past.

9

Forgive the Comment That My Passion Made

"It's beginning to look a lot like Christmas. Toys in every store. Tiddley-tiddley pom." Since hearing the song on Monday evening, he had not been able to get those nonsensical lyrics out of his head. Barry laughed at his off-key singing as he drove from Ballyholme to Holywood for a light lunch with Sue. Light because he knew from experience how large would be the buffet table at the Sports Club's Christmas party later in the day.

The Driscolls' cottage was right on the way, and last Friday Barry'd promised someone would pop in late this morning to see if Jill could go to the party this afternoon and meet Santa. He turned onto the narrow road leading to the cottage, tapping the steering wheel in time to the tune still playing in his head, and parked Brünnhilde outside.

Mrs. Driscoll must have heard the car because before Barry could lift the elephant's trunk knocker, the front door was opened. She smiled at Barry. "Good morning, sir. Fine day." She looked up and Barry, hearing the cries of "pee-wit, pee-wit" overhead, followed her gaze to see a stand of green plover, a peculiar term he had always thought, considering how their flight pattern staggered across the pale blue sky.

"Pretty birds. I've always called them plover, but Declan calls the wee birds lapwings," she said, inhaling. "He's a grand fellow for the birds, so." She took another deep draught of air. "Warmer than the last few days we've had."

"It is. But there's snow in the long-range forecast."

"Is there, indeed? Well, a white Christmas would be lovely and Jill's never seen snow."

"How is she?"

"Come and see for yourself. I think you'll be pleased. I can find nothing but scabs." She stood aside to let Barry enter. "In the front room."

Jill was sitting at the kitchen table in a red dressing gown dotted with white rabbits. As he came closer, he saw she was using crayons to colour a Christmas scene of Santa and his eight reindeer headed by Rudolph with an enormous red nose. Barry was suddenly reminded of Ballybucklebo's undertaker, Mister Coffin. The poor man suffered from rhinophyma, a blockage of sebaceous gland ducts that caused swelling and redness of the nose-tip. "Hello, Doctor Laverty. Look." She held the book up for him to see. "I'm trying to keep inside the lines."

"And you're doing very well."

She smiled. "And Mammy says my rash is doing very well too. You've come to see it, haven't you?"

Barry had to smile at the eagerness in her voice. "I have. Mammy? Please."

In moments Mammy had stripped Jill down to her knickers.

"Please stand up, Jill."

Barry examined the child from head to toe. Glory be. Not a single vesicle left. Every last one had scabbed up. Barry reckoned he was feeling nearly as excited as Jill was going to be when he said, "Mammy, may I suggest you don't bother with nighties and dressing gowns. Please help Jill put on her party dress." He watched the little girl's eyes widen, her mouth drop open, her smile grow, and he heard her laughter turn the air happy. "You're going to the party—and Santa's going to be there."

Jill danced a little jig and clapped her hands.

The tears ran through Mrs. Driscoll's smile. "Come on, *muirnin*." She took her daughter's hand. "Can you wait for a minute please, Doctor? I've a shmall-little thing for you, but it's chilly. I'll get Jill dressed first."

"Of course. I'm not in a hurry."

"Please have a seat."

He settled himself into an overstuffed chair by the fire. A small Christmas tree decorated in old-fashioned, homemade ornaments in one corner already sheltered some brightly wrapped parcels underneath. Sprigs of red-berried holly lay on top of picture frames and were scattered along the mantel among quite a few Christmas cards. Clearly her friends and family in Cork knew her address.

The turf was spluttering, so he popped up to give it a good poking and chucked on another piece. A small wisp of smoke leaked into the room just as Mrs. Driscoll and Jill came back. She had had her hair neatly done up in two bunches and was wearing a knee-length sky-blue woolen dress with long sleeves, white knee socks, and shiny black patent leather shoes.

"My," said Barry, "don't you look pretty?"

Jill blushed and nodded. "Fank you very much."

Mrs. Driscoll must have noticed the smoke. "Mister Gilligan phoned today. He'll be here to sweep it at midday on Boxing Day. He's sorry he can't come sooner."

"I'm glad to hear it," Barry said. He paused, aware of the

sound of a car slowly approaching, then stopping. A car door was slammed, and he and Mrs. Driscoll stood silently waiting for the inevitable knock on the door. Mrs. Driscoll frowned. "Who could it be?"

She started when three short raps on the door echoed through the quiet house.

"You're about the only living soul we know in these parts. Perhaps Mister Gilligan found he could come earlier." She opened the door, shrieked, and stepped back with her hand over her mouth. "Holy Mother of God. Declan." A short, dark-haired young man entered and closed the door behind him. "What the hell are you doing here?" Her eyes blazed.

Jill raced across the room and threw herself at her father. "Daddy. Daddy."

As a wide-eyed, trembling Finella slumped into a chair, Declan Driscoll picked up and cuddled his daughter. "Hello, Jilly, love. Daddy's come to take you and Mammy home to Bandon."

Barry moved to be near Finella, feeling concerned and a bit guilty. Kinky had been very clear in the instructions she had relayed to Barry yesterday from her brother, Tiernan. Let Declan's arrival come as a surprise. It had certainly been that. "Are you all right, Mrs. Driscoll?" The woman's face was white and for a terrible moment, he wondered if they'd done the right thing. What, after all, did we really know about this man?

Declan stood carrying a giggling Jill and walked quickly to where Barry stood beside Finella Driscoll's chair. The man smiled and nodded at Barry, who stepped back as the man crouched by the chair, his daughter on his knee. His gaze sought his wife's eyes and then held them. "I'm sorry, Finella," he said, "please listen. I'm truly sorry about what happened. I shouldn't have got legless."

"No, you shouldn't." She sat up more firmly." "And it wasn't for the first time with your bowling *spailpins*—och—" She shook her head rapidly.

He hung his head. "But it'll be the last time. I promise." He reached out a hand and touched her arm. "I should have apologised right there and then, so. That's what I'm doing now. I was wrong, dead wrong, and I am truly sorry."

"Truly?" Barry heard hope in the young woman's voice as she looked at Declan's face. "Really and truly?"

"Yes. Really and truly. Can you forgive me? Will you and Jill please come home with me to Bandon? Please? I've missed you and I love you both so much."

Finella narrowed her eyes, inhaled, looked down and back up at Declan. She pursed her lips, inhaled through her nose, then spoke. "You just said you promised it would never happen again." She shook her head. "How do I know it's not a piecrust promise. Easily broken?"

Declan hung his head.

Barry thought he understood. There was no real answer to that question.

She said, "Damn it all, man, I was sixteen when we met. I've never looked at another man . . ."

"Nor me at another woman."

"We had something extra special." There was a crack in her voice.

Barry saw Declan's eyes start to glisten before he said, "I know. And I've come close to throwing it away . . ."

Jill wriggled from her father's arms and stood. "Mammy, please. I don't understand what you're arguing about. I don't care about seeing Santa. I wanna go home, Mammy. I want to go home with Daddy and you."

"Just wait a wee minute, pet." Her voice was steady as a rock. "If you'll promise to behave and really mean it, Declan, mean that it won't ever happen again, so?"

"Cross my heart." He did as he spoke. "As God's my witness, I do love you both so much. Please come home."

Barry waited for what seemed like an age until at last, keeping her voice level, Finella said, "All right. All right. Yes. I think so. I'll give it another try." She nodded and was smiling as she turned to her estranged husband. "But what in the name of God provoked you to come now?"

"My road bowling friend—"

At those words Finella stiffened. "What kind of friend keeps a man away from his wife and family?"

"Listen to me, pet. You don't understand. Tiernan O'Hanlon's sister is housekeeper to Doctor O'Reilly in Ballybucklebo." Declan looked up at Barry. "Is that you, sir? Are you Doctor O'Reilly?"

"No, I'm his assistant."

"I see. Well, Tieran's sister phoned and asked Tiernan to make me see sense. I was being thran, stiff-necked, and too stupid to see it. But Tiernan, he's a good man, Finella, he talked sense into me. It's going to be all right now, so." He leant forward and kissed her.

Barry was delighted when after a moment's hesitation, the kiss was returned and a tearful Finella said, "I do still love you, Declan Driscoll, you, eejit."

"And Daddy's back. Daddy's back. Never mind Santa," sang Jill.

Finella rose, kissed Jill. "Is Daddy going to stay for Christmas? We've a tree, Declan. We have presents. There may even be some for you." She smiled and inclined her head in his direction.

"Yes, I am. And we'll all see Santa today."

"Hooray." Jill wriggled back into her daddy's arms and he kissed her cheek. "I love you, Daddy."

"Who's my good girl?"

"Me."

Finella watched and smiled. "And I still love you, Declan, you unmitigated bollix." She took a deep breath. "And I accept your apology, but if it happens—"

Declan set Jill on her feet quickly and held out his hand, palms up. "It won't. I promise." He pulled Finella to him and kissed her long and hard. "I promise."

Barry saw a look of wide-eyed awe cross Jill's face. "Right," he said, feeling warm, happy, and relieved that things had turned out so well. Finella had not needed the emotional support he thought she might, and no one needed him here now. "I'll be running along, but I'll see you all at the party."

"Party?" said Declan. "I'm your man."

"You'll have to be a sober one," Barry said. "There'll be kiddies there, so no alcoholic drink permitted." At least not officially, he thought, but Constable Malcolm Mulligan always turns a blind eye to weak mulled wine.

Declan laughed.

"Just a minute please, Doctor," Finella said. She went to the tree, lifted a wrapped, bottle-shaped parcel, and handed it to Barry. "That's a wee something from Jill and me and now Declan too, so." She turned to Declan but was smiling when she said, "Just because you're cut off, Driscoll, doesn't mean you are, sir. It's from the Driscoll family, the just made whole again family, to wish you and yours a merry Christmas, and a happy New Year, so on the day you can raise a glass."

"Thank you very much," said Barry, accepting the gift. "And you've given me more than a bottle. You've let me enjoy your excitement, Jill, and share in the happiness you two must be feeling. I don't think I'll get a better present and my merry Christmas has started already."

Full of warm feelings for the Driscoll family, Barry stopped at the Ballybucklebo traffic light and looked up at the decorated maypole's festive finery. He had a sudden recollection of last year's Christmas party. Like the Driscolls this year, Gerry and Mairead Shanks's family had been new in Ballybucklebo last year and had brought their two children, Angus and Siobhan. The convention was that parents brought wrapped and labelled presents for their own children to put in Santa's sack. No one had thought to tell the Shanks. But Fingal had saved the day. He usually did and the little ones had not gone without presents.

After what had recently happened at the Driscolls', it had not been the time to explain to them about buying toys, but Barry had a plan. Medicine wasn't the only thing he was learning from O'Reilly.

He drove on when the light turned green, found a parking spot at the side of the road, and crossed to Cadogan's newsagent's shop. Among their usual wares they stocked a small collection of toys.

The shop was closed for lunch, but the family lived above

the shop and didn't mind being interrupted. He rang the bell, heard a clattering of footsteps on the stairs, and was greeted by a smiling Phyllis Cadogan.

"Doctor Laverty? Don't tell me it's an emergency and Doctor O'Reilly's run out of his favourite Erinmore Flake pipe tobacco?"

"Not at all, but it is a kind of emergency. The Sports Club's Christmas party is this afternoon . . ."

"Come on on in." She stepped aside and opened the door to the shop. Instead of the tinkling of a bell that usually announced the arrival of a customer, the first few bars of "Jingle Bells" rang out. She followed Barry. "Let me guess. Someone's coming to the party and there's no Santa present for them. Sure, didn't I charge back here to try to get a couple last year for your Doctor O'Reilly to put in his Santa sack? Wee boy or girl?"

"A little girl."

"I've got just the job." She led him past newspapers, magazines, bottled sweeties, cigarettes, and tobacco until she stopped in front of a shelf laden with Dinky toy cars, water pistols, dollies, and stuffed puppy dogs. "Here." She handed him a slim, cellophane-wrapped book entitled, *Dress-a-Dolly*. "Wee girls love this, so they do. It comes with a cardboard dolly who's only wearing her knickers. They've to cut her out. Blunt-nosed scissors are included in the package and then every page of the book is a different outfit to cut out and dress the dolly in."

"Marvellous," Barry said. "I'll take it. How much?"

"Five and six."

He smiled. "Cheap at half the price," and handed over two half-crowns and a sixpenny piece. "Thanks, Phyllis. I tell you what, give me a tin of Erimore Flake and," he knew how much Sue liked them, "a box of Rowntree's Black Magic dark chocolates."

She filled his order, put it in a paper bag, accepted his payment, and made change to the accompaniment of a loud "ting" as the cash register drawer opened. "Here you are. So, are you just doing a last-minute gift run for Doctor O'Reilly or will you be able to be at the party, too, Doctor?"

Barry anticipated the look on little Jill Driscoll's face when she met Santa and he handed her her present. "Phyllis," he said, "I'd not miss it for the world."

10

Winter Afternoons

Barry stood before the front door of the Ballybucklebo Bonnaughts Sports Club and pointed to the huge holly wreath. "Beyond this door lies Christmas mayhem. Are you ready, Miss Nolan?"

Sue laughed, beginning to unbutton her coat. "I'm ready, Doctor Laverty. I can hear the kiddies right through the door."

Together they went through and into the warmth. The level of noise seemed to Barry on a par with the racket of riveting at Harland and Wolff's shipyard in Belfast. Danny Kaye's version of "All I Want for Christmas Is My Two Front Teeth" roared from a loudspeaker system.

They hung their coats in the cloakroom and surveyed the scene. Children were running about like lilties, screaming, laughing, and yelling. People had to shout to be heard over the music and the children. "Come on," he said taking her hand. "Let's join the party." He held a parcel wrapped in Christmas paper. "And the first thing I want to do is get this to Fingal, so Jill Driscoll won't be left out when Santa hands out the Christmas presents. I see him up there." He pointed to a table at the far end of the crowded main hall.

The pair's progress past packed tables was slow. Sue as a local school mistress and Barry as a GP were known to everybody and stops to exchange seasonal good wishes were frequent. Tobacco smoke blued the air and mingled with the savoury smells of roasted meat and the sweet smells of mulled wine and Christmas baking.

Danny Kaye's childlike voice rose over the clamour. Colourful streamers hung in loops from the ceiling. The huge Christmas tree stood glittering in one corner, its fairy lights flashing. Beside it an empty armchair awaited Santa and beside it stood a bulging sack. Kiddies kept charging over to admire the tree and stare at the sack and giggle.

Barry and Sue were halfway to their destination when they stopped at two trestle tables. Behind one, a beaming Kinky Kincaid stood with her helpers, Cissie Sloan, Flo Bishop, and Aggie Arbuthnot, who was famous for having six toes on each foot.

"Merry Christmas to you all, ladies." Barry surveyed the tables. "Good Lord, but you've been busy. "Mutton, turkey, beef, ham, wheaten bread, pan loaf. What a feast." Dotted among the huge cold roasts were colourful salads and side dishes.

"My friends here looked after the roasts. I did the dried dates stuffed with marzipan, the chocolate-covered cherries, and the sweet mince pies." She pointed to the other table, laden with desserts.

Barry smiled. "You are to be congratulated. All of you."

"Thank you, sir." She looked over Barry's shoulder, "If you'd excuse me, I think we have some customers."

Barry turned to see Ballybucklebo's arch trickster, Donal Donnelly with his shock of carotty hair and buck teeth, hand in hand with his wife, Julie. "Merry Christmas, Donnellys."

"And a happy New Year to you and Miss Nolan," Donal said as they parted, the Donnellys to partake of the feast, Barry and Sue to carry on.

Danny Kaye finished and for a while the sound level dropped until Frank Sinatra's mellow tones began the song, "Have Yourself a Merry Little Christmas."

Barry felt a tugging at his sleeve and turned to see Jill Driscoll and her mammy and daddy smiling at him. "Hello, Doctor Laverty. Hello, Miss Nolan."

"Hello, Jill." Barry crouched down until he was level with the little girl. "So, what do you think of the parties we throw here in the wee North?"

"It's better than anything. Thank you for letting me come," and then with the guilelessness of her six years, Jill asked Barry, "Is Miss Nolan Mrs. Laverty? She's very pretty, you know."

"Isn't she?"

"Barry," Sue said, but she was smiling and eyeing Finella.

"And no, she's not Mrs. Laverty." But, Barry thought, when the time was ripe, he was going to ask her to be.

Jill jumped and skipped. "And I'm going to see Santa."

"Soon, Jilly. Very soon," said her father.

Barry looked up and saw the Driscolls smiling and nodding. Declan said, "She's been talking about nothing else since you left, Doctor."

Barry said, "Daddy's right, Jill. He will be coming soon." He glanced over to Kinky. "Come with me. There's someone I'd like you all to meet before Santa gets here." He led them back to the buffet. "Excuse me, Kinky. Could you spare a minute?"

She came out from behind the table.

"This is Mrs. Kincaid who has a brother Tiernan down in . . ." Barry paused.

"Béal na Bláth," Declan said. "Mrs. Kincaid, I don't know how to thank you. I'm Declan Driscoll."

Kinky's grin was vast. "And you must be Finella, and you're

Jill. From Bandon, so." She took Jill's hand. "How would you like a cherry dipped in chocolate?"

"Ooh. Yes, please."

"Well go and get one. After you've seen Santa, there'll be some boring grown-up stuff. But once it's over, I'll introduce you to some other boys and girls if Mammy and Daddy would like that?"

Declan said, "Grand, so." He took Finella's hand. "You go on with Mrs. Kincaid, Jill. We'll wait for you—"

But Kinky and the little girl had already turned and were making their way to the dessert table without a backward glance. Declan smiled and shook his head. "Thank you, Doctor. I do think Jill is lonely for little ones her own age."

"I'm sure she is," said Sue. "But Kinky will soon put that to rights."

She and Barry moved on, continuing their slow progress through the hall. "You were quite right about Finella Driscoll. She is lovely. And her husband let her move all the way up here over something to do with a silly game?"

Barry laughed. "Not just a game, Sue. It's road bowling. And I think it was a bit more complicated than that."

"I'm sure it was." She shook her head. "Men."

Barry reached for her hand, squeezed it, and leaned over to give her a kiss on the cheek.

When he saw them, O'Reilly stood up from where he was seated beside Kitty. "Barry. Sue. Good to see you both. I think you both know Councillor Bertie Bishop and Fergus Finnegan, who are members of the executive."

Barry said, "Mister Bishop. Fergus."

They replied.

"Doctor Barry Laverty and Miss Sue Nolan, I'd like to present you to Lord John MacNeill, Marquis of Ballybucklebo, his sister, Lady Myrna Ferguson, and their brother, Mister Andrew MacNeill, recently returned from Australia."

Barry bowed and said, "My lord, my lady," he straightened, "and Mister MacNeill."

Sue dropped a small curtsey.

"Now," said O'Reilly, "come on, you two, and sit down."

Barry turned to Sue. "I just need a quick word with Fingal," and nipped over to him, handed him the wrapped parcel, and said sotto voce, "Her parents didn't know the form about their needing to have a present ready, so here's one. She's my patient who missed a trip to see Santa on Saturday and nearly didn't get a second chance today. Make it extra special for her, please."

"I will," said O'Reilly. "I nipped over to Cadogan's earlier to get a couple of extra presents just in case. Phyllis told me you'd been." He accepted the parcel and quickly stuffed it up under his coat. "Good man, ma Da. You're a quick learner."

"Thanks, Fingal." Barry looked at Sue and felt his heart lifted by both the sight of her and the praise from O'Reilly. Christmas 1965 was beginning well.

Bing Crosby began crooning Irving Berlin's "I'm Dreaming of a White Christmas."

Sue had found a seat beside Kitty, leaving one between herself and Lord John MacNeill, which Barry took.

The marquis leaned over and said to Barry and Sue, "In private, I'd be pleased if you would call me John—"

Myrna interrupted, "And I'm fine with Myrna in public."

He smiled at his sister. "I'd like to be as informal as my sister, but I'm of the opinion that one must keep up appearances, at least in public," he said. "But constant 'my lords,' or 'your lordships' become wearisome for everyone. I prefer 'sir.'"

"I understand, sir," Barry said.

Sue nodded. "Thank you, sir."

"Good. Now, if you'll excuse me for just a moment, I need a quick word with Fingal and Bertie.

"Bertie, thank you for agreeing to introduce my brother to the club and thanking him for his donation in 1951."

"My pleasure, sir."

Andrew was scanning the room and then stopped. Barry looked over to where his gaze had landed.

"Just recognized a very old friend. I'm itchin' to talk to him. It's been a long time, but I suppose I'll have to wait a little longer."

"That reunion will have to come later," said the marquis. "All eyes need to be on Santa. Fingal, you know what to do now."

"I've been doing it since 1947, sir, when you first asked me to." O'Reilly grinned, rose, and headed toward the office to change.

The old groaner's 1951 recording of "Christmas in Killarney" was cut off in mid-stream, O'Reilly's cue to make his entrance, just as it had been last year. "Ho-ho-ho. Merry Christmas," he said to himself, remembering that as well as children, Saint Nicholas was patron saint of mariners, bankers, and pawnbrokers. He didn't think there were any pawnbrokers here tonight, but there were certainly mariners and bankers. But Christmas was the children's time and seeing their joy when Santa spoke to them and gave them a gift was one of his great pleasures.

He strode out of the office, now resplendent in his red suit trimmed with white fur, conical hat, matching tunic and trousers, black shiny belt, and black knee-boots. His clip-on white bushy beard tickled.

Opening the door to the main hall, he bellowed, "Ho-ho-ho. Merry Christmas."

Cheers greeted him and redoubled in volume as he made his way through the room. O'Reilly, with his back to the crowd, fumbled under his tunic and put Jill Driscoll's present into the sack at the top. Barry's words came back, "Make it extra special for her," and O'Reilly already knew what he was going to do. He climbed into the chair and roared, "Ho-ho-ho. Lovely to be back in Ballybucklebo. Now who's been naughty and who's been nice?"

The noise of conversation faded.

He caught sight of Donal Donnelly's red thatch. "Don't answer, Mister Donnelly. Judging by your record, I know I'll have a lump of coal for you."

With Donal's well-earned reputation as a confidence trickster, the response was exactly as O'Reilly had anticipated. Gales of laughter. And good natured as he was, Donal joined in, then said, "With all the ones you've given me over the years, Mister Claus, I'll have enough now til start my own coal business."

O'Reilly waggled his finger at Donal as the hall erupted into more laughter. "Now," said O'Reilly once it was quiet again, "Ballybucklebo's not the only place I've to visit, so let's see what's in this big sack, shall we?"

"Yes, please, Santa," said the kiddies in unison.

"All right. Children, when I call your name, come up or have Mummy or Daddy bring you up to receive your prezzy." He stood, turned, and looked into his sack. When he turned back, he held a wrapped gift. "Jill Driscoll?"

The crowd applauded.

He scanned the crowd. There. A little girl in a long-sleeved blue dress with her hair done in two bunches was coming forward holding her mother's hand.

They stopped in front of him.

The little girl sucked her thumb. Her blue eyes were wide and shining as she stared at him.

Mother hunkered down beside her daughter. "Don't be scared, Jill. Santa has a present for you. Say hello to Santa."

Out came the thumb. "Hello, Santa. Thank you for coming from the North Pole."

O'Reilly handed her the present. He sighed. "It wasn't easy. The elf who was to help me has the chickenpox."

Jill Driscoll's eyes were round with wonder. "I had that too. Poor elf. It's awful."

He frowned at her, then smiled. "I'm glad to see you're all better now. Would you do me a big favour?"

"Yes, Santa."

"Would you be my helper now?"

Jill's mouth formed an O. Her eyes widened. "Can I, Mammy? Can I?"

Finella said, "Give me your present. I'll mind it for you, and say, 'Thank you, Santa. Yes, please.'"

Jill handed over her parcel. "Fank you very much, Santa. Yes, please."

Finella said, "Thank you, sir, very," with heavy emphasis on the *very,* "much."

"All right, Jill. This is what I want you to do. Come over to my toy sack over here." He led her to it. "Put in your hand and pull out a present."

As she did, he retook his seat. "And bring it to me. Thank you. Now stand over there." He indicated the right-hand side of his chair. While she took her place, he read the label and called, "Ho-ho-ho, Billy Cadogan, get you up here this very instant."

Billy came up like a flash. "Thank you, Santa." He left.

Together O'Reilly worked with his helper until the sack was empty and every child had been given a gift. During this time, he'd been aware of people coming and going from the buffet. He grinned and hoped Kinky had remembered to set aside a morsel or two for a now very hungry jolly old elf.

O'Reilly stood and took Jill's hand. He called, "That's it. I'll see you all next year, but now I need to go to my store for my next run and before I do, I want a round of appreciation for my wonderful helper, Jill Driscoll, who hails from County Cork."

The room erupted in cheers, whistles, and clapping.

He looked down at Jill who was hopping up and down, and to Jill's mammy who had tears running through her wide smile. "Thank you, Santa. You've given a very happy little girl a present she'll never forget."

11

A Bridge of Reconciliation

O'Reilly threaded his way through the tables and made a beeline for the door to the office amid more cheers, whistles, and clapping. There, praise the Lord, he could shed his heavy Santa suit. The sweat trickling down his forehead was obscuring his vision and he nearly tripped over an electric floor polisher. He heard a woman's voice he recognized behind him. "Santa, wait for me, please."

He stopped. "Myrna?" He half-turned. "Myrna?"

"Yes. I need to talk to you."

"Come on then."

She hurried along and he had already opened the office door by the time she had drawn level. "Come in."

As soon as she entered, he closed the door, indicated one of two plain chairs in front of a desk for her, and started to unbutton his tunic. "Unless you're haemorrhaging or having a heart attack," off came the tunic revealing a set of red braces over an undervest, "let me get out of some of this gear first." Off came the beard. "I'm baking." He blew out his breath, reached into the hold-all in which he had brought his Santa suit, and hauled out a towel. After his first year as Santa he'd always brought one. He towelled his mop of dark hair, wiped his face, fished out a comb from his suit jacket, which with his shirt, tie, and trousers was hanging on a peg, and combed his hair. "Oh boy, that's better. Just let me get out of these boots too."

Even with the main hall and office doors shut he could hear,

> Jingle bells, jingle bells, jingle all the way, oh what fun . . .

O'Reilly took the other seat. He smiled at Myrna. "Sorry to ask you to wait, Myrna. What can I do for you?"

She frowned, stared at the top of the desk, pursed her lips, inhaled, looked straight at O'Reilly, and shook her head.

Whatever it was, it was troubling her deeply. He waited.

"It's about Andrew." She swallowed. "It's all my fault."

O'Reilly knew to be patient.

A single tear leaked from the corner of Myrna's left eye. She dashed it away with the back of one hand, leaving behind a smudge of mascara, and muttered, "Pull yourself together, girl," before continuing. "Fingal, I've been unfair to my own brother all my life, and I'm sorry for it." She hung her head, before looking back up at him. "I know he led a wild life when he was younger. I despised him for that." Her voice hardened. "But damn it all, he's a MacNeill. He had obligations to the family. We all do. That's how I felt." She swallowed. "I really let that show on Friday night, and I'm sorry."

"We can't always control how we feel about things. Sometimes when we get really angry with someone near to us it's a reflection of how much we care about them."

She cocked her head to one side. "Do you mean that?"

Fingal rested his lower jaw on his left thumb, curled index finger on his chin.

She nodded. "You do. I can tell. Thank you."

"Go on, Myrna."

"I've been doing a lot of thinking since Friday. Since my outburst, we've avoided each other. Been civil when needed, but that's it. I have no doubt my brother is a flawed human being, but aren't we all?"

"You know I'm not much of a religious man, but I seem to remember Christ saying, 'He that is without sin among you, let him cast the first stone.' Gospel of Saint John, 8:7."

Myrna managed a tiny smile. "So do I. We learned it at Sunday school. But it's more than that. My remark about Andrew's illness as divine retribution was unforgivable. Despicable. He is a very sick man, isn't he?"

"Yes, he is. Right now, he's in remission, but he will require periodic blood transfusions. When the disease worsens—and it will but God knows when that will be, it could be years—there's a chemotherapeutic agent called chlorambucil and steroids that will help for a while. Who knows what other advances will be made?"

"I see. I think that's promising. But what I said earlier about his actions—that he's a MacNeill and had obligations to the family. I've come to realise it's a two-way street. I'm a MacNeill and I have obligations to my family—and that includes brother Andrew."

O'Reilly leaned back in his chair. "You are a remarkable person, Myrna. I applaud you."

Her smile was self-deprecating. "I've been a scientist for too long not to face facts." Her look held supplication. "I want to try to make amends, but I'm not sure how to start. Can you help me, Fingal?"

O'Reilly thought. Amends? Yes, and the sooner the better. "I think I can. You'll want privacy, so I suggest we go back to the party, wait until the speechifying's done, then I want you to come back here. There's someone Andrew wants to see so I'll come with him and I'll bring Andrew here soon after and leave you two alone."

"No." He heard an edge back in her voice. "I want you to stay, Fingal. I may need help."

"Very well."

"But what am I going to say?"

"I don't think it's for me to advise you, Myrna, but I will say you've convinced me of your sincerity." He smiled. "You'll find the words. I know you will." He rose. He noticed her mascara. "You might want to go to the ladies' now and I need to get out of these red trousers and into my ordinary clothes."

"All right," she said, and as he passed her chair she stood and hugged him. "You are a very good friend, Fingal Flahertie O'Reilly. Thank you."

Dashing through the snow, in a one-horse open
 sleigh, o'er the hills we go . . .

O'Reilly let himself back into the party where conversations were drowning out most of the music. As he began passing one table, he overheard Gerry Shanks, sitting by his wife, Mairead, talking to his friend Lennie Brown. "You mind last year your Colin was the innkeeper in the Christmas pageant and he wouldn't let Joseph in?"

"Aye. I was mortified. I thought we'd never live it down—but it was a bit of a gag right enough." He laughed. "Poor wee lad couldn't come tonight. Bloody chickenpox. Connie's keeping him company."

"She's a good woman, and he'll be over it soon."

"Aye. Right enough on both counts."

O'Reilly knew he should get back to his table, but the doctor in him couldn't stop himself from asking, "And, how is he?"

"He's starting til scab up nicely, Doctor, and he says it's not so itchy."

"I'm glad to hear it."

"But we've had hell's delight trying to keep him indoors and away from his mates I can tell you. It being Christmas and all." Lennie lowered his voice, "By the by, you was a wheeker Santa, sir."

"Thank you, Lennie. I've looked forward to it every Christmas since '47."

O'Reilly was about to leave, but Gerry said, "Hang about, Doc. I was about to tell Lennie and Mairead what happened in Holywood last night. You'll enjoy this. You was there when Colin pulled his prank last year."

O'Reilly nodded.

"I hear they had the opposite at their Holywood pageant. 'It's Mary and Joseph,' says Joseph. 'Can we come in?' and the Bethlehem innkeeper says with a big grin, 'Aye certainly. Come on, on in. I've the bridal suite ready for youse.' When I heard that I laughed like a drain, so I did."

O'Reilly could not contain his own guffaw. "That's terrific. I think I'll have to tell Sue Nolan about that. Excuse me now."

"Off you go, sir." Lennie Brown lifted his glass of mulled wine. "Season to be jolly, all right. Cheers."

And Gerry returned the toast.

O'Reilly chuckled and moved on to see Kinky beckoning to him. He went her way. She looked around to be sure there were no children nearby. "You were a grand Santa, Doctor. Grand, so."

"Thank you." He inclined his head to the trestle tables. "Lord, would you look at that. You'd think one of the plagues of Egypt had been here when the skinny cows ate all the fat cows. There's only enough bones to interest an archaeologist where those lovely roasts used to be, and not a sweet thing left at all."

"Just a minute, sir." Kinky bent and pulled out a plate from under a tea cloth. "I saved you some turkey, mutton, ham, some salads, and though I shouldn't, it's Christmas so there do be two sweet mince pies for your dessert."

"Bless you, Kinky. You may just have saved a life."

"Run you along, sir. Mrs. O'Reilly has cutlery and a glass for you too."

O'Reilly set a course for his table while Dean Martin, sounding as ever slightly tipsy, crooned, "Walking in a Winter Wonderland."

"Welcome back, Fingal," Kitty said.

He noticed that Myrna, makeup renewed, had beaten him to the table.

O'Reilly immediately started tucking in.

"You were the best Santa ever." Kitty handed him a glass of mulled red wine, which he raised just as Constable Malcolm Mulligan in civvies walked by deep in conversation with Mister Christopher Coffin, the undertaker. They stopped at O'Reilly's table and PC Mulligan said, "My lord, my lady, and the table, a very merry Christmas."

Lord MacNeill replied on behalf of his group and glasses were raised. Before the police officer left, he remarked, winking at O'Reilly, "Enjoy your Ribena, Doctor."

"I will, Malcolm. I will."

"You're on now, Bertie," the marquis said.

"Right, your lordship—sir." The nearly spherical councillor

and worshipful master of the local Orange Lodge got to his feet, adjusted the loops of gold chain of his fob watch, and began walking to the stage.

The marquis turned to O'Reilly. "Bertie, of course, was on the committee in 1951 when we were raising the money. I brought him up to date when Andrew phoned me ten days ago. The executive has had a plaque engraved. It's on the lectern for presentation and will be hung in Andrew's honour tonight." John MacNeill looked over at his brother, who was laughing at something Kitty had said. "I still can't quite believe he's here, Fingal. I never thought I'd see my brother again."

"He's here, sir. He's home."

Bertie climbed up on the stage and went to the lectern and microphone. He tapped it twice and the buzz of conversation faded. He leaned to the mike and said, "Can you hear me at the back?"

From a table near the door, the widower Alan Hewitt, who had brought his pretty, red-headed daughter Helen, yelled back, "They can hear you in Donaghadee, Councillor."

Polite laughter.

Bertie stood straight, hooked his thumbs into his waistcoat pockets, and said, "My lord, my lady, ladies and gentlemen, first of all, on behalf of the executive may I wish you all a very merry Christmas and a happy and prosperous 1966?"

Applause.

"And now to come straight to the point. You may remember in 1951 we had a drive to raise funds for a complete renovation of this here clubhouse, so we did. You all know that an anonymous donor put up half the money."

There was a subdued murmuring.

"That donor, who has returned to Ballybucklebo after a long absence in Australia, is with us tonight. Will Mister Andrew

MacNeill, brother of the Marquis of Ballybucklebo and Lady Myrna Ferguson, please come up here?"

A questioning buzz began.

O'Reilly watched a smiling Andrew rise without assistance, cross the floor, and hop up on the stage, plain evidence of how much good his recent blood transfusion had done him. He stood beside Bertie.

Bertie lifted the plaque. "Mister MacNeill, on behalf of the executive and all the members of the Ballybucklebo Bonnaughts Sports Club, it gives me great pleasure to present you with this plaque as a token of our thanks for your most generous donation. It reads, 'This plaque is to express our deepest gratitude to Mister Andrew MacNeill for his magnificent donation toward the renovation of this clubhouse in 1951. A gift within the bounds of the long tradition of generosity to Ballybucklebo by the MacNeill family.'" He handed Andrew the plaque and stepped aside.

Andrew immediately stepped in front of the microphone and before anyone could applaud, had raised his hand. There was silence. "I'll be brief. I-I . . ." He paused to clear his throat. "I find I do not have the words to express my thanks for this plaque, nor my pleasure in seeing how my gift has been put to work to help modernise this wonderful building. Earlier this evening my brother was kind enough to give me the conducted tour. It is wonderful, truly wonderful, to be home again in Ballybucklebo." He lifted the plaque above his head.

A photographer from the *County Down Spectator* took a series of flash photographs.

Bertie spoke into the mike. "Three cheers for Mister Andrew MacNeill. Hip, hip, hip . . ."

O'Reilly had thought the thunder of his old battleship *Warspite*'s fifteen-inch rifles had been the loudest sound in the world. After the third cheer, he thought he might have to revise his opinion.

As Andrew handed the plaque back to Bertie for immediate hanging by Donal Donnelly, carpenter by trade, O'Reilly noticed Myrna excusing herself and heading for the door. He quietly said to Kitty, "Myrna wants me to try to effect a reconciliation between her and Andrew. I'm going to let the smoke and dust die down here a bit then take him to her."

"Oh, Fingal, that's wonderful news. I've been chatting with Andrew while you were Ho, ho, hoing. I could become quite fond of that man. He's overcome by being back home at last. The welcome to the village he's just had must have tickled him pink, and if Myrna is willing to make up, I think he's going to be the happiest man in Ballybucklebo tonight."

The volume of conversation in the room had almost reached its previous level but, presumably, because the afternoon's DJ was attending to his plaque-hanging duties there was no piped music, for which O'Reilly, finishing his last sweet mince pie, was grateful. "Right. I'm off." He excused himself and went to where Andrew had resumed his seat and was chatting to Barry and Sue. O'Reilly waited until the conversation had come to a natural conclusion and said, "Congratulations, Andrew."

The man's smile was beatific. "Thanks, Fingal. Thanks for everything. And I'd like to be able to thank whoever donated the blood I received at the hospital on Monday."

"Sorry, but you can't. Like the donation you made to the club in '51, it was made anonymously."

"God bless them anyway, I'm a new man. Now the formalities are all done, there's someone I want to talk to."

"So, are you fit for a short walk now then? I'll come with you. There's someone I'd like you to talk to as well."

"Of course." He rose. "We'll be back in a minute or two."

"Take your time," Sue said. "I'm sure there are lots of people who would like to meet you." She turned back to Barry, Kitty, and the marquis.

O'Reilly and Andrew threaded their way toward the door but fetched up at a small table where Sonny Houston and Maggie Houston née MacCorkle were sitting. She was formally dressed. She had her false teeth in and a sprig of holly in the band of her red felt hat.

Sonny leapt to his feet, shook Andrew's hand, and embraced him in a monstrous hug, before putting one hand on each of Andrew's shoulders and stepping back to stare into his eyes. "Andrew MacNeill. Welcome home. It's been thirty-nine years since you went off to seek your fortune in Australia. Welcome back to Ballybucklebo. Welcome back to Ireland."

Andrew was misty-eyed. "Sonny. Stone me, but it's so good to see you. I'm sorry I couldn't come over earlier tonight."

"And given the number of folks visiting your table, Santa's doings, and then the presentation, we didn't seem to be able to get a chance to come to you. But you're here now."

"I'm here now," Andrew said softly, then brightened. "Looking at us two old codgers, it's hard to believe the pair of us rowed for Cambridge in 1924."

Sonny laughed. "And we beat Oxford."

"A fact I think you've mentioned in every letter we've exchanged since then. You know, Doctor, the two of us have kept up a correspondence ever since."

O'Reilly smiled. His guess about Andrew's mysterious local informant had been correct.

"It is delightful to meet you in person, Maggie."

Maggie cackled her wind-in-dry-leaves laugh. "Those were

the most beautiful opals you sent me when thon ould goat and me got wed last year. Thank you again."

"How long are you home for?" Sonny asked.

"I'm not sure. I do have to get back to Australia in the New Year, but we'll get together properly soon."

O'Reilly said, "There'll be a small at-home at Number One Main Street from eleven to one on Christmas Day. The MacNeills will be there. If you and Maggie—"

"We'll be there," Sonny said. "Thank you, Doctor."

"And I'm sorry to break up this reunion, but there is someone I really would like Andrew to talk to, so we'll see you on Christmas Day. Andrew? Coming?"

O'Reilly stopped outside the office door with Andrew, who was still grinning, and knocked.

It was opened by Myrna. "Come in, Andrew. Fingal."

"Myrna?" Andrew's face fell but he went in.

O'Reilly closed the door.

"Please have a seat, Andrew. There's something I want to say."

Andrew parked himself on one of the chairs. She took the other. He sat half-turned and hunched, with one shoulder facing her.

His face was blank when he said, "Myrna, I don't need another dressing down. Today has been one of the best days of my life. Please don't spoil it."

O'Reilly flinched. He knew Myrna MacNeill of old. Ever ready to go on the defensive—the best method of which was to attack.

"Andrew," and her voice was soft, "Andrew. I didn't persuade Fingal to bring you here so I could chastise you. You hardly know him. I do. If I had, he'd have told me to do my own dirty work."

Andrew frowned but his shoulders relaxed a little.

"I wanted to talk to you in private with Fingal here for support because this is difficult for me." She took a deep breath, hesitated, then the words rushed out. "But I want to apologise."

"To apologise? Good God. To me?"

"Yes. To you. We were never close in the past, I admit I disapproved of you, and I'm not stupid enough to shed crocodile tears for what is over and done."

"That's all right. I understand."

"But when John told me ten days ago that you were sick and wanted to come home to Ballybucklebo I found I was still angry. So stupidly angry that it didn't even occur to me that I had a golden opportunity—we," she paused, "had a golden opportunity to start over."

"I see." His shoulders relaxed some more.

"And I want you to understand that your illness is not why I feel this way. It's not a false sympathy thing. I'm very sorry you are sick, but I'd be just as sorry for my actions if you were fit and well. To state this quite plainly, I have been terribly wrong."

Myrna had never been one to varnish the truth.

"You are no less my brother than John. We are all MacNeills, and I love you both." She panted a little as her words rang out.

"Myrna." Andrew stood. "Thank you, sister. Thank you." He took her hand and helped her to her feet.

O'Reilly looked away as Andrew took his sister in his arms, for their family tears should be a private thing, but in his heart, he felt, leukaemia in remission notwithstanding, this was going to be the merriest of Christmases for the clan MacNeill.

12

Fluting a Wild Carol

When he heard the front doorbell ring, O'Reilly looked up from reading an old favourite, Herman Wouk's *The Caine Mutiny*. "Kinky will see to it," he said to Kitty who was on her knees by the now-decorated spruce trying again to dissuade Lady Macbeth from batting with her front paw at a low-hanging red glass ball.

"Who could that be?" she said, leaning back on her heels.

O'Reilly knew the caller was unlikely to be a patient at two-fifteen on the afternoon of Christmas Eve. "Everyone knows the surgery's closed." True emergencies would phone and be redirected to the Contactors Bureau.

"Doctor and Mrs. O'Reilly," Kinky's voice came from below, "I think you should come down and see this."

O'Reilly was on his feet at once. He knew after all these years that she wouldn't summon them unnecessarily and he had a notion who it might be. "Come on, pet."

Together they hurried downstairs to where Kinky held the front door open.

Cissie Sloan, whose musical talents went beyond her virtuosity on the harmonium, stood with her back to the front steps. Facing her and the front door, arranged in a shallow arc, were Eddie Jingles, Billy Cadogan, Aggie Arbuthnot's daughter Hazel, Dermot Fogarty, Irene O'Malley, the twins Carolyn and

Dorothy Kyle, Jeannie Kennedy, and Micky Corry. Those two had been Mary and Joseph in last year's Christmas pageant. Every child held a paper booklet. All were neatly dressed and bundled in overcoats, scarves, gloves or mittens, and woolly hats against a nippy wind that the sun, just past its solstice point, did little to moderate.

O'Reilly had guessed correctly.

"Now, children," Cissie said. "On three." She blew into a pitch pipe. "One, two, three."

Sweet soprano and treble voices sang out in unison.

We wish you a merry Christmas,
We wish you a merry Christmas,
We wish you a merry Christmas,
And a happy New Year.

O'Reilly watched the delighted smile spreading on Kitty's face. As the little choir worked up to their request for figgy pudding and a cup of good cheer, he thought of the scene in Kenneth Grahame's *The Wind in the Willows* where the dormice sang carols for Water Rat and Mole.

Finally came the demand:

. . . We won't go until we get some so bring it out
here.

Kitty was applauding and laughing. Fingal joined in.

"Very good, so," Kinky said. "Now, I've no figgy pudding, but I do have gingerbread men and in no time at all I can make hot chocolate, so if you'll all come into my kitchen? You must be perishing."

O'Reilly and Kitty stood aside as a chorus of "thank you" sounded in the hall and Cissie and the choir trooped past. O'Reilly was approached by Micky Corry who held up a collecting can labelled SAVE THE CHILDREN. Two folded one-pound notes found their way through the slot in the tin's top.

"Thank you, Doctor O'Reilly."

He closed the front door behind them.

Cissie Sloan was in full cry, her reputation as the most talkative person in the village and townland secure. "Now Kinky, how did you find the new people from County Cork? I saw you chatting to them on Wednesday at the Sports Club party. I thought the little girl was very pretty, so she was, and her ma, Finella, isn't it? Gorgeous altogether. Do you think they'll stay in the North? I heard Finella's grandma was some sort of wise woman. I never went to see her, but I know folks who did. All sorts of strange medicines she was after making . . ." Her voice faded as the little group went into Kinky's kitchen and the door was closed.

As he and Kitty climbed the stairs, O'Reilly said, "This is the second year that little choir have made Number One Main their last stop. They know well enough that Kinky will give them treats. Last year she told them a ghost story about growing up as a girl in County Cork and having a brush with the Irish fairies, the people of the mounds." He realised he'd never mentioned Kinky's special gift to Kitty. "Kinky's fey, you know."

"No. You mean she has the sight? Can tell the future?" Kitty laughed. "You really believe that?" She disappeared into the upstairs lounge.

As he turned into the room he heard, "Bloody cat," and immediately saw why. Seven shiny glass balls now lay on the carpet. The little cat had been gentle. None were broken. But every lower branch had been stripped. Lady Macbeth lay in front of the fire with a green ball against her tummy looking satisfied with her work. Kitty was down on her knees picking the others up. She shook her head but smiled at him. "I think I'll concede defeat. That's the third time her ladyship has done it."

"Fine by me," he said, stooping to help. He glanced at his watch. "Ten minutes until the BBC broadcast of the nine lessons and carols from King's College Cambridge. This'll be the first time I've listened to it with you, pet."

She smiled at him and blew him a kiss. "And I can promise you it won't be the last."

O'Reilly looked with satisfaction at the remnants of Kinky's roast duck breasts. The sage and onion stuffing, roast parsnip, and roast potatoes that had accompanied it had all been finished. A mere smear of the accompanying apple sauce remained in the small bowl.

Kinky appeared carrying a tray. She set a Waterford cut-glass bowl on the table. "This is my ma's recipe. Sherry trifle." She began to clear off. "And how was the duck? My ma in Cork when I was little always served our family goose or salted beef on Christmas Eve. Of course, a whole goose would be a bit much for two people."

Kitty said, "It was delicious. Thank you, Kinky."

O'Reilly recalled that in Nelson's navy, the crews subsisted on salted beef and salted pork. He'd prefer roast goose or roast duck anytime.

She inclined her head to the trifle. "Some folks serve trifle on Christmas Day, but I believe the Christmas puddings should be kept until tomorrow." She lifted the now-full tray. "I'll be back with the Christmas cake when I come to finish clearing the table." She left.

O'Reilly tucked into the trifle. "Mister Robinson, the Presbyterian minister here, calls sherry trifle 'the parson's last hope.' Many congregations, not his thankfully, expect their man of God to be an abstainer but are quite prepared to ignore the sherry in the trifle."

Kitty shook her head. "I should hope so."

"Which reminds me—what would you think about going to midnight mass? Ballybucklebo is a pretty ecumenical place and I must say I find the Roman mass a moving experience. I try to go most Christmas Eves. Last year Barry and Kinky came with me. They enjoyed it."

Kitty nodded. "I've never been to a Catholic service. I think I would enjoy it too," she said. "It probably wouldn't hurt to be reminded why we celebrate this season. Yes. Let's."

"It's what Christians do. I like to think about all the cultures that celebrated midwinter with festivals this time of year. The Romans had their Saturnalia, the early Celts marked the winter solstice with Yule, in Japan I think they lit big bonfires on Mount Fuji." He refilled both their glasses from a chilled bottle of a crisp Gewürztraminer.

By the time they had finished their trifle, Kinky had reappeared with coffee, After Eight dark chocolate mints, and an iced and decorated Christmas cake and cake knife. She set them on the sideboard.

"If you are going to Mass, sir, when you come home, you'll want to open the cake like you always do, so."

"I will." He sipped his wine. He'd never understood why

cutting the first slice was referred to as "opening" the cake, but it was traditional to do so on Christmas Eve. He asked, "And will you be going with Flo Bishop, Kinky?"

"I will, sir. Archie will meet us there. Bertie will give Flo and me a lift, although he'll not be at the service—"

O'Reilly chuckled. A Catholic chapel was no place for the Worshipful Master of the staunchly Protestant Orange Lodge.

"—once I have the house cleaning finished."

Kitty frowned. "House cleaning? Kinky, some folks call this time of the year the holidays and you're cleaning house. This evening. Really? You've done a marvellous job getting ready for our at-home and Christmas dinner tomorrow. The house is spotless. Can't you take a break?"

Kinky shook her head and smiled. "There does be a reason. Christmas was, of course, when a baby came into Bethlehem in Judea and He and His parents had no place to stay except a stable. When He comes again, and He will, Irish country people want to be sure the house is prepared to greet Him. We also leave a candle burning in the window to light His way."

"I didn't know that, Kinky. I'm such a city girl." Kitty sat back. "I'm learning a lot tonight. I hope you don't mind me asking. Earlier Fingal was telling me you have the sight, but he didn't get a chance to explain. Do you? Can you see into the future?"

Kinky's voice dropped and O'Reilly felt as if a chill had come into the room. "I do, as did my ma and her ma before, so. And it does be more of a curse than a blessing. I've often no idea what it is I'm seeing or what it means. I just had a blurred sight earlier this afternoon when Cissie Sloan was going on about the new family from my own county of Cork. The little girl is going to be very happy tomorrow on Christmas Day." She nodded to herself.

Kitty said, "But surely that's a good thing?"

"It is." She took a deep breath. "But I see tears on Saint Stephen's Day, what northerners call Boxing Day—and for the life of me I cannot see why."

The bells rang in Saint Columba's steeple. O'Reilly could picture the ringers hauling on the bell ropes. Outside, the Nativity scene was illuminated and the stained glass in the three pointed-arch windows glowed brightly from the light coming from within. O'Reilly had lately developed a unique connection to those windows. To replace the ancient original ones, these had been installed in 1939 by a stained-glass craftsman working in the modern style of Wilhelmina Geddes. The world-famous stained-glass artist happened to be aunt to Doctor John Geddes, who, along with Doctor Pantridge of Belfast's Royal Victoria Hospital, had introduced the world's first cardiac flying squad just two months previously.

He and Kitty passed under the high-arched, oak front door.

Incense filled the air. Ahead of them, Alan Hewitt, followed by his daughter, dipped their fingers in holy water, crossed themselves, and genuflected toward the altar.

O'Reilly and Kitty entered the packed chapel and he led her into the back pew beside the Hewitts, where the O'Reillys both bowed to the altar and were seated. As he would have done in the Presbyterian church, he closed his eyes and bowed his head. All those years of rigid discipline at school, two services every Sunday, and divinity classes, had given him a solid grounding. He murmured a short prayer, concluding, "In the name of the Father, Son, and Holy Spirit." He then straightened up and opened his eyes.

Alan said, sotto voce, "Good evening, Doctor and Mrs. O'Reilly. Nice to see you here."

"Thanks, Alan," O'Reilly said.

The chapel was small, intimate. The chancel was separated from the nave by three low steps, at the top of which was the communion rail. Behind it to the right was a dark wood lectern, to the left the pulpit. The communion table, immediately behind the low wooden railing, was flanked by two five-foot-tall wrought-brass candlesticks. In each, a large white candle flamed. Candles seemed to burn everywhere.

A boy treble began singing the first verse of the traditional processional hymn a capella. "Once in royal David's city stood a lowly cattle shed . . ."

The congregation rose.

O'Reilly half-turned to see Father Hugh O'Toole lead the processional up the central aisle.

The priest's red cope had a gold seam running up the centre from the cloak's hem to its collar, and was crossed at shoulder height by a narrow gold strip reaching shoulder tip to shoulder tip. Beneath he wore a white surplice.

Behind him came two altar boys in white surplices. Each swung a smoking censer. The choir followed, six boy trebles, including Dermot Fogarty, who had sung the solo first verse, and Micky Corry, four altos, eight tenors, and four basses. They wore white robes with scarlet ruffled, high collars.

Father O'Toole stopped just before the altar rail, turned, and faced the congregation. His right arm was outstretched above his head. The choir filed into their stalls behind the altar rails.

> "And He leads His children on, to the place where He
> has gone."

The hymn ended and as all the Catholics present crossed themselves, the priest made the sign and said, *"In nomine Patris, Filii, et Spiritu Sancti."*

In the name of the Father, Son, and the Holy Spirit. O'Reilly had no difficulty understanding. As a student at Trinity College Dublin School of Physic in the 1930s, he had attended one lecture a week delivered in Latin.

He joined in the communal "Amen," and sat with the rest of the congregation.

The service continued with a greeting, an invitation to partake in an act of penitence, and a communal confession, starting with the words *"Confiteor Dei omnipotenti, beatae Mariae semper Virgini . . ."* I confess to almighty God, to blessed Mary ever Virgin, and ending with *"mea maxima culpa,"* . . . my most grievous fault.

Father O'Toole gave the prayer of absolution.

O'Reilly, ever the traditionalist, understood how adherents to the faith could find comfort in the Latin. And comfort in acknowledging their faults and receiving forgiveness. He smiled. He was not unconscious of his own faults, but forgiveness? He shook his head.

The congregation responded in song, *"Kyrie, eleison . . . Christe eleison . . ."* Lord have mercy upon us, Christ have mercy upon us.

O'Reilly looked around at the backs of the heads of familiar people. Donal Donnelly's carroty tuft beside Julie's gold. Miss Moloney's pepper and salt. He smiled when he noticed Archie and Kinky. She was beside her best friend, Flo Bishop.

Beside them were the Reverend Robinson and his wife. He would lead the Presbyterian service on the morning of Christmas Day. Reverend Robinson and Father O'Toole were close friends, and years ago the two men had agreed to disagree over some matters of dogma, agreed on the fundamentals of Christianity, fostered ecumenism in the village and townland—and golfed together every Monday afternoon.

"Gloria in excelsis Deo, et in Terra pax hominibus bonae voluntatis . . ."

Glory be to God on high, and on earth peace to men of goodwill . . . And wouldn't it be wonderful, O'Reilly thought, if the peace to all men and women of goodwill could last all year round?

". . . adoramus te, glorificamus te."

. . . we adore thee, we glorify thee.

The *Gloria* ended and silence reigned for several moments. A perfect moment of absolute tranquility in a chapel that had stood here for centuries.

After a short prayer, a lay reader, a man O'Reilly recognized by his bulbous red nose as Mister Coffin the undertaker, walked to the pulpit and read from the book of Isaiah. "For Zion's sake I will not keep silent, and for Jerusalem's sake I will not rest . . ."

He listened to the old words from the King James Bible. ". . . and behold a virgin shall be with child, and bring forth a son, and they shall call his name Emmanuel, which being interpreted is, God with us . . . and knew her not till she had brought forth her first-born son: and he called his name Jesus."

When the time came, neither O'Reilly nor Kitty took communion. They watched the procession to the altar rail, the reverence of the communicants as each received the bread and the wine.

O'Reilly felt different. At peace. Content. He closed his eyes and took a deep breath. An image of wee Jill Driscoll popped into his mind and he let his mind rest for a moment on that little nagging concern of Kinky's for the girl. No. He took another breath and let the silence and peace settle his mind. He would not worry. Today was Christmas Day. He would trust that all would be well and that he could enjoy it to the full.

Father Hugh concluded the service and dismissed the congregation with the line, *"Ite, missa est."* Go, you are dismissed.

O'Reilly rose with the rest and joined lustily in the recessional hymn.

> "God rest you merry gentlemen, let nothing you
> dismay,
> Remember Christ our Savior was born on Christmas
> Day . . ."

Because they were in a rear pew, O'Reilly and Kitty were among the first to leave the church.

As they stepped out into the dark night, the chill nipped at his face. Yet O'Reilly's heart was warmed by the joyous pealing of the bells above.

He saw Kinky, Archie, and Flo being helped by Bertie into his van. Kinky would be back at Number One Main before O'Reilly and Kitty.

He took his wife's hand and, passersby be damned, gave her a smacking kiss. "Merry Christmas, my love. Home, Christmas cake, a nightcap, and bed."

She laughed and he saw that the peace of the service in the old church showed on her face. "Merry Christmas to you, my dear old bear. That sounds very good, because with an at-home in the morning and Christmas dinner in the afternoon, it's going to be a busy day."

13

Christmas Morning Bells Say, "Come"

"You can come into the house," said O'Reilly to Arthur Guinness as he let the big Lab into the back garden, "but only until ten forty-five. Our guests will be arriving by eleven and we can't have you underfoot, sir. I'm sorry, but it can't be helped. You're just too big."

Arthur regarded him with a baleful look. Not for the first time, O'Reilly was convinced the dog knew exactly what he had said and, in this case, was not impressed. Normally Arthur spent all Christmas Day in the house, but this was the first time, now that O'Reilly was married, he had invited a few select friends for a festive drink after many years attending the open house at the marquis's estate. "Don't worry. It'll only be for an hour or two."

O'Reilly had risen early, well before sunrise, but with sufficient light to take Arthur for a walk to Ballybucklebo Beach. Before setting off, he had given Arthur his Christmas present, a great marrow bone and had let him gnaw on it for a few minutes.

Now, as Arthur passed his doghouse, he wagged his tail, then stopped and looked at his master. O'Reilly reckoned the dog's look was wistful.

"Kinky will definitely not be over the moon if I let you bring that thing into her kitchen." O'Reilly continued walking and, after a moment, the dog followed. "Don't worry, it'll be waiting for you when you get back. Go on in now," he said, opening the kitchen door and leaving behind the grey morning. There may be snow in the long-range forecast, but there would not be a white Christmas this year.

As ever the kitchen was toasty, and redolent of the smells of ham, turkey, and two kinds of stuffing all cooked the previous day and resting in the cool pantry. The turkey and its gravy would be ready for reheating immediately before today's dinner. The ham would be served cold. O'Reilly knew Kinky would be preparing the roasted and mashed potatoes, Brussels sprouts, and bread sauce today, and that everything would be perfectly cooked.

Kinky turned from where she was preparing sausage rolls. "Good morning, Doctor, Arthur. *Nollaig shona, agus Dia duit.*"

Arthur, with a deep sigh, lay down in front of the range.

"And merry Christmas and God be with you too, Kinky." He bent over the stove and took a deep draught of the mouth-watering smell. "I'm curious. What's bubbling?"

"It do be the pope's nose—"

"The what?"

"Oh, sir, I'm sure I've told you this before. I'm making the stock for today's turkey soup. It's a very useful bird."

O'Reilly laughed. "Of course, the giblets. But what in the name of the wee man is the pope's nose?"

"It's that bit of the neck that's left after the butcher has removed the head. That and the giblets make a marvelous stock."

"Well, it all smells delicious. Is Mrs. O'Reilly up?"

"She is, sir, and in the dining room having her coffee. I do have some grapefruit and nice poached eggs for breakfast for you both."

"Lovely. And are you going to church this morning?"

"I am. Archie will meet me there at five to ten. It's a short service so we'll be back at Number One well before your guests start to arrive, so." She turned back to her task. "Now run along, sir. I can't make eggs until you've had your grapefruit so get started before Mrs. Kitty thinks that's all she's getting for her Christmas breakfast, so."

"I will." O'Reilly nipped along to the dining room door, stuck his head in, and said, "Morning and merry Christmas, pet."

Kitty smiled at him. "Merry Christmas, Fingal. Did you enjoy your walk with Arthur? It's a grey sort of day but not too cold."

"A bit chilly out, but Arthur and I have had much worse wildfowling on Strangford Lough. And we had the place to ourselves. I think for a lot of dog owners Santa takes precedence today, and speaking of that, you start, dear. I'll just be a minute." He didn't wait for an answer but took the stairs two at a time, lifted four parcels from under the tree, and headed down.

"Merry Christmas," he said, and set the parcels on the table close to where Kitty sat.

"Thank you, Santa dear. I've poured your coffee," she said, "so get stuck in. You know how Kinky dislikes people not eating her food."

"All right." He drank some coffee and, using a spoon, lifted the first segment of grapefruit to his mouth, puckered, and reached for the sugar bowl. "Tangy," he said and put two teaspoons of sugar on his portion. "Much better. Now, why don't you open your present? It's the long one."

"Fair enough." Kitty found hers and began ripping the paper

open. "Oh, Fingal. A portable outdoor easel. And it's a beauty." She traced her hands across the grain of the polished wood. "I don't have one." She blew him a kiss. "Thank you. It's lovely and there are so many wonderful landscapes to paint in County Down. Wait a minute, there's something else." She ripped open the last of the wrapping and peeled back layers of tissue to reveal a white box edged in black. "A bottle of my favourite perfume, Je Reviens. You really are a dear, thoughtful old bear."

He inclined his head. As ever he was embarrassed by praise, even from his wife of nearly six months.

"Thank you, Fingal. Now, you've finished your grapefruit, you can have your present." She handed him his parcel.

It was heavy, wrapped in red-and-green-tartan paper, and tied up in a huge green bow. He slipped off the bow and tore open the paper. Two large books. He looked at the title of the first, gold letters on a green cover, *Wild Chorus*. And the second, the blue-covered *Morning Flight,* both by the naturalist, master painter of wildfowl, and author Peter Scott, only son of Scott of the Antarctic.

A quick glance inside revealed that both were inscribed with Scott's unassuming signature. For a moment O'Reilly, keen wildfowler that he was, was speechless. "I've always wanted them, Kitty. And autographed? Thank you, darling. Thank you very much."

"You are very welcome, my love. Perhaps one day you'll take me to Strangford Lough, and you can shoot, and I can paint?"

"Only in September if it's mild. For most of the wildfowl season, Strangford's as cold as a—" He bit off what he was going to say. "Very cold."

She laughed as Kinky came in asking, "Are you all done?"

"Yes, thank you, Kinky." O'Reilly pushed aside his plate,

"But before you start clearing off, take a gander at those two parcels."

"Two parcels, sir?"

"One from Kitty and me and one from Doctor Laverty."

"Oh." She lifted one. "This one's from you and Mrs. Kitty, sir." She carefully took off the wrapping paper and folded it neatly. "It'll come in handy next year," she said to herself. "Waste not, want not." She opened a tall white cardboard box and removed a lady's pearl-grey hat. "Oh, my. It does be very elegant, so." She turned it in her hands, admiring it.

"I asked Miss Moloney's advice," said Kitty, "and I am quoting her description. 'It is a one hundred percent wool Bardot fedora with a three-inch medium brim, a pinched crown, and a black grosgrain band.'"

"It is beautiful." Kinky had a wicked little grin. "I'll wear it to church this morning. It'll take the light from Flo Bishop's eyes, so it will. Thank you both so very much." There was no malice in Kinky's words about Flo, just a hint of friendly rivalry.

O'Reilly chuckled. "Health to wear it. Now let's see what else you've got."

Kinky paused to read through the tag on her other parcel and laughed. "It is from Doctor Laverty, so. He says he knows how much I love to cook, and that Archie may not be one of the great chefs of all time. So, when he and I get wed in April, Doctor Laverty wants me to have some of the very best kitchen utensils." She began unwrapping the parcel with the same care she'd unwrapped the first one.

"He dropped it off yesterday so you could have it this morning before our guests arrive."

"Very thoughtful of him, sir," she said. "And—Jasus, Mary,

and Joseph, did you ever see the like?" She showed them a case containing a set of Sabatier top-of-the-line chef's knives. "I do not believe Fanny Craddock would own the like." She shook her head, "He's a darlin' man, Doctor Laverty, so. A darlin'."

"You'll be able to thank him soon," Kitty said.

"I will." She had taken one of the knives out of the box, a wickedly sharp-looking meat cleaver, and was running a finger along the steel.

"That's a powerful-looking implement," O'Reilly said, noting how time was passing. "You'll need to be getting ready for church. And I believe there was some rumour of poached eggs?"

"By the hokey, I was so pleased with my gifts I quite forgot." Kinky carefully returned the knife to its box. I'll leave my presents here for now." Then she cleared off quickly and fled.

O'Reilly guffawed. "That speaks volumes. You know how proud she is of her meals."

"She really is pleased. I'm delighted."

In a very short time, the eggs on toast had been delivered and eaten, and Kinky stuck her head into the dining room. "I'm off now. Archie and I will be back soon to look after the at-home and Christmas dinner."

O'Reilly called back, "We'll tidy up, here. See you soon."

He reached out his hand to grasp Kitty's, and as Kinky and Archie left through the front door, they could hear the chapel bells' joyful chorus summoning the faithful.

"I can still feel the peace of sitting in that lovely old chapel last night, Fingal. I'm glad we went."

"So am I."

The faint sound of the bells continued, and they sat, hands clasped, listening until Kitty looked at her watch.

"Mum's spending today with her sister, my auntie Jessie, and her family in Carrick on Shannon. "I'd like to give her a quick call. Can you start clearing off, pet?"

"Go right ahead." O'Reilly stood and started stacking dishes ready to take to the kitchen.

As he passed Kitty, he heard her say, "Yes, everybody's fine at this end too. I just called to wish you a merry Christmas and a happy New Year from Fingal and me to everyone there. And our love . . ."

When she joined him, he was up to his elbows in hot soapy water. She was smiling. "My lot are all well and send love and season's greetings. Now, let me give you a hand."

O'Reilly let Arthur out into the back garden. "We'll have you back when they've gone, old fellah. Enjoy your bone." He closed the door and turned to Lady Macbeth. The upstairs lounge would soon have all kinds of tasty nibbles on tabletops. Far too much temptation for a young cat. "Wait you a minute, girl, until I open your Christmas present." Last year she'd wolfed down some tinned anchovies. The fishmonger had not had any in stock so this year O'Reilly had canned sardines, which he hoped would make up in part for her temporary banishment. He spooned one onto a saucer and set it on the floor beside her usual feeding bowl. "Merry Christmas, your ladyship," he said. "Enjoy that."

He watched her whiskers twitch as she sniffed at the saucer, took a pace back, and looked at him with scorn in her gaze. Uh-oh. He imagined he could hear her thinking, "You surely don't expect me to eat that stinking thing covered in oil?" She'd have been scenting turkey and ham since yesterday. He laughed.

"All right, you'll get a bit of both when they're carved, but for now you're staying here with your sardine." He let himself out and closed the door behind him just as the front door opened and Archie and Kinky let themselves in. "Merry Christmas, Doctor," Archie said as he helped Kinky off with her coat and her new hat.

"And how did Flo like your fedora, Kinky?"

"She was most complimentary. Said I had a powerful taste in hats, so."

14

Death Hath No More Dominion

"Coming," O'Reilly bellowed, trotted down the hall, and opened the front door to find his elder brother, Lars, standing on the top step, his arms full of packages.

"I know I'm a bit early, Finn, but the roads from Portaferry were practically deserted."

"I'm not surprised on today of all days." The two men stood grinning at each other and O'Reilly decided his brother, at fifty-eight, was looking well. He was a little taller than O'Reilly and his thick hair and pencil-thin moustache were still dark.

"Well, don't just stand there with both legs the same length. Come in, come in. And merry Christmas, brother."

"Merry Christmas, Finn." Lars juggled his packages as O'Reilly helped him shed his coat, and the two brothers went upstairs, to be greeted by Kitty who was sitting beside a gently glowing coal fire.

"Kitty, as always you are looking lovely," said Lars. O'Reilly agreed. Her oyster-white dress with its skirt of close-set pleats suited her well.

"Now," said O'Reilly, "let us unburden you of those packages."

"This is for you, Kitty, and one for Finn." He handed Kitty two gaily wrapped parcels, took a seat by the fire, and set a third parcel at his feet as O'Reilly headed to the tree to retrieve the one for his brother. "Go ahead, Kitty."

Kitty quickly undid the paper and opened a small, pearl-grey velvet box. "Oh, Lars, you shouldn't have. It's beautiful." She showed O'Reilly an antique cameo brooch. "Thank you."

Lars smiled, "For a beautiful lady. Yours, Finn, is perhaps self-evident, or as we lawyers say, *'Res ipsa loquitor'*—the thing speaks for itself. Open it."

Even by its feel, it was clearly a picture. O'Reilly ripped off the paper. He stood so he could prop the framed and glazed work against his chair. "Would you look at that?" He stood back and gazed at a scene of a stream flowing past low banks under a mackerel sky with one patch of blue. Between it and the stream, a large ragged V of pale-bellied Brent geese flew from left to right. "I remember Uncle Hedley, who taught us to shoot, had one of these Peter Scott prints. It was done in 1937." He turned, beaming at Lars. "Where the hell did you find it?"

Lars glanced at Kitty. "Your lovely wife recommended a little antique shop in Greyabbey."

"Conspiracy," O'Reilly said with a vast grin. "Thank you both. Thank you very much." He handed Lars his gift. "Now, your turn."

Lars unwrapped his. "My God, it's *The Orchidaceae of Mexico and Guatemala* by James Bateman. An old orchid-growers' guide I've always wanted." He flipped through the pages and gestured to the parcel beside him. "For Kinky. It's a pair of gloves to go with the hat I happen to know she got this morning. I hope she likes them as much as I like my gift. Thank you both."

O'Reilly went to the bottle-and-glasses-laden sideboard, and asked, "Kitty? Lars?" Two glasses of Harvey's Shooting Sherry, less sweet than their famous Bristol Cream, were soon poured as well as a small neat John Jameson for himself.

The three were just settling into their chairs for a chat when Kinky bustled in, Archie at her heels, both carrying trays. "Excuse me, sir. Oh, Mister Lars. Merry Christmas, sir. Doctor, seeing there'll only be ten of you, it has not been a big job to cater and nobody will want to eat too much with their dinners to follow, so."

As usual Kinky had excelled herself in the assortment of hors d'oeuvres.

O'Reilly watched as sausage rolls, mushroom patties, smoked salmon on wheaten bread, chicken liver pâté on toast melba, cheese-stuffed dates wrapped in bacon, and dried figs, along with plates and napkins were distributed on tabletops, the mantelpiece, after space had been made among the Christmas cards, and even the closed lid of his gramophone. It was closed for a reason. O'Reilly disapproved of the modern idea that every social event must be accompanied by background music. He found it intrusive and forced everyone to shout to be heard above the noise of it.

"Archie will greet the new arrivals and send them up, and I'll be getting on with preparations for dinner later, so. When everyone's here, he'll come up and take over serving drinks from you, sir, and circulate with plates."

"Thank you both very much," Kitty said. "The food looks beautiful, Kinky."

"It's all the old favourites, so. People like the traditions this time of year. Now, we'd best be getting back to the kitchen."

"Before you go, Kinky." Lars rose and handed her the parcel. "Merry Christmas."

She bobbed and smiled. "Thank you, Mister Lars. Thank you very much. I'll save it until this evening when Archie and I have our dinner."

O'Reilly said, "Do me a favour, please, Archie. Pop that picture in the TV room. Don't want it getting knocked about."

"Certainly."

"Thank you."

"So, Finn?" Lars asked, retaking his seat once Kinky and Archie had returned to the kitchen. "Was Santa good to you? I have no doubt he was good to you, Kitty."

"He was. Very."

O'Reilly, meanwhile, had removed two books from the shelf and showed them to Lars, who also was a keen wildfowler. He whistled. "You are a lucky devil. You know some of the pictures in here were painted on Strangford?"

"There's one of Brent geese done in oils on canvas I know about and—"

"That's right. You own a print of it now, pet."

"You two were really in cahoots, weren't you?"

"Guilty as charged," said Lars seriously, looking very much like the lawyer he was. Then he laughed, a deep, rich, baritone sound that reminded O'Reilly of their father. "What a tonic it is to be here today. Finn, Kitty, enjoy your gifts and—"

"Hello, O'Reillys. Merry Christmas." John MacNeill stood at the doorway of the lounge, his tall, erect figure filling the space. "Permission to come aboard, Commander. Mister Auchinleck sent us up."

"John, Myrna, Andrew, come in," O'Reilly said, putting the books back on the shelf. "Permission granted. Merry Christmas."

"Lars, it's good to see you again. I don't believe you know Myrna, my sister, or my younger brother, Andrew, who is visiting from Australia?"

Lars inclined his head. "How do you both do?"

Replies were made.

O'Reilly took the drinks order and as he poured, he took a good look at Andrew. Unless someone knew his medical history, there was no reason to suspect he was an unwell man, but the doctor in O'Reilly decided it might be best for Andrew to find a chair now. He couldn't recall who had called this kind of cocktail party 'Perpendicular Purgatory,' but the description often came true and it would be unreasonable to expect Andrew to stand for the duration. He stared at Kitty and inclined his head to Andrew.

She nodded.

He handed Andrew an eggnog, nonalcoholic of course, and Kitty called, "Andrew, come and sit beside me. I want to hear how your visit's going."

Andrew smiled at his sister and the smile was returned before he said to Kitty, "I wish to God I'd come home years ago. I've got a wonderful family."

Barry and Sue, immediately followed by Sonny and Maggie Houston, appeared, and Archie whispered to O'Reilly, "That's everyone, sir. I'll take over the drinks."

"Thank you, Archie."

O'Reilly watched as good old Maggie, who had honoured the special occasion by wearing her teeth, bobbed a curtsey to the marquis. She was wearing a very jaunty black felt hat with a large deep red rose tucked into the hatband.

"Did Mister Houston give you that rose, Mrs. Houston?"

"He did, your lordship. You wouldn't think to look at him, but my Sonny's a grand one for the romantic gestures."

"The beauty of the flower, the red rose that stands for love, cannot surpass that of the lady who wears it," Sonny said.

And Kitty clapped her hands. "Well said, Sonny."

"Ould goat," Maggie said, but the depth of her feelings shone through.

"Good for you both," said O'Reilly, then, "Does everyone have a drink?"

A chorus of "yes" and "yes, Doctor," filled the room and all eyes turned to him. "Thank you, everyone, for I'd like to propose a toast."

He raised his glass. "Thank you all for coming to our home on this Christmas Day, 1965. This is a special one for me because it's the first one I am spending with my new bride. Kitty, thank you for making this one of the happiest Christmases of my life. Let's drink to a very merry Christmas and for every one of us a happy, healthy, and prosperous New Year."

Nine voices returned the toast.

"Good," he said. "Thank you. The occasion has been duly honoured and now as Lars and my old elementary teacher used to say, 'Talk nicely among yourselves.' If you need another, Archie will attend to your order," and to illustrate his next remark he put a sausage roll, two pieces of smoked salmon, and one piece of chicken liver pâté on toast melba on a plate. "The nibbles are plentiful so please help yourselves." Once he'd fortified himself with some of Kinky's delicious hors d'oeuvres he wandered over to have a word with Barry and Sue, who were seated by the Christmas tree.

"Sue, you are looking ravishing." And she was, her long copper plait shining in the daylight that streamed in through the bay windows, her eyes sparkling like the fairy lights on the Christmas tree. She was a very happy young woman.

"Thank you, kind sir."

"Fingal," Barry said, "I hope you and Kitty are having a good Christmas."

O'Reilly laughed. "We are. It's good to have a bit of time off, but I'll expect you back at work on December the twenty-seventh and I've been saving this up for you for today. Happy New Year. As of January, the first, you will be a full partner." He offered a hand. "Congratulations, Barry."

Barry stuttered, "I-I—wow," collected himself, and shook O'Reilly's offered hand vigorously. "Thank you, Fingal. I could not have asked for more this Christmas."

Sue was more demonstrative. She stood and kissed his cheek. "Fingal O'Reilly," she said. "I know Kitty calls you her old bear. I think you are Teddy, Paddington, and Winnie the Pooh rolled into one." She turned to Barry. "Congratulations, darling."

O'Reilly could almost see the love that flowed between the two youngsters. Ah, to be young again, he thought. And yet, didn't he feel the very same way about Kitty, could feel that love flowing whenever he looked at her. He was a lucky man, to be feeling this at the ripe old age of fifty-six. He smiled at them. "I'm the lucky one. I couldn't wish for a better medical partner. Now enjoy yourselves." He wandered over to where Andrew was chatting to Sonny and Maggie. "Hello, folks. I hope you're enjoying yourselves."

"Enormously," Sonny said. "I never thought I'd live to see my old rowing friend again, much less be having a drink with him on Christmas Day. He's told me, with no details about what ails him, how you've been looking after him, for which I thank you, Doctor."

O'Reilly shrugged, "Isn't it my job?"

"Yes, technically," Andrew said, "but you've treated me like a human, not a disease."

O'Reilly bowed his head.

"And it wasn't your job, Sonny, to maintain our correspondence over all those years. If you hadn't, I'd not be here in

Ballybucklebo." He smiled at Maggie. "I feel fortunate to have had the pleasure of meeting you at the party and now here, Maggie."

"It's me that's proud to know you, Andrew, so I am, and that's why we're having you for lunch tomorrow. It'll be like everyone else's. Leftovers. But you'll get a chance to try my fruit cake."

O'Reilly had to hide a shudder. Maggie's fruit cake was infamous for being as impenetrable as *Warspite*'s armour plating. "You'll enjoy that, Andrew," he said, crossing his fingers behind his back.

"There is something I need to tell you, Sonny and Maggie. I didn't get a chance yesterday. Doctor O'Reilly knows."

O'Reilly frowned, but said nothing. He noticed that Barry and Sue had drifted over to join Kitty, John, and Myrna.

Andrew inhaled. "I didn't tell you yesterday because I needed a little longer to think about it, and please, it's not as bad as it sounds, but I have leukaemia."

Maggie's eyes widened.

Sonny's face crumpled. "I'm so sorry, Andrew. We'd no idea it was something serious."

"Please don't be. Doctor O'Reilly has explained to me that if one is going to have leukaemia, the kind I have is the least serious. Still serious, mind you, but there's hope. I've had most of this week to think about it. I've had a blood transfusion and physically I feel wonderful. My family here in Ballybucklebo and my medical advisors know all about it. It is only right that my friend of longest standing and his wife should know too."

"We appreciate that, Andrew," Sonny said.

"And if there's anything we can do, just ask," Maggie said.

"Thank you both. It is very comforting to be here with my Irish family and friends and I apologise for giving you a shock just now." He looked around the room. "Christmas can be such a joyous time and here I am, I'm afraid, a bit of a spanner in the works. People may be trying not to show it on the outside, but inside I'm sure you're all feeling sad for me. So, I have a little announcement I'd like to make to the company. If you'd all follow me?" And he set off toward the fireplace and the others. Sonny and Maggie and O'Reilly followed.

In moments the full party was together with Andrew facing them. "My family and friends, old and new, there's something I'd like to say to you all."

Archie, who had just refilled Myrna's glass, said, "If you'll excuse me, I'll go downstairs and see how Kinky's getting on." The man nodded to O'Reilly and he nodded back.

To O'Reilly, Archie was not the least out of place at this point in the gathering. But the man was being tactful, sensitive, O'Reilly thought. Kinky had got herself a good one there.

No one else spoke. Everyone was looking at Andrew.

"I'll only be a minute, but there's something important I'd like to say to you all. Fingal. Kitty. Thank you both for inviting me into your home."

"Our pleasure, Andrew," Kitty said.

"Lars, I hope I'll get to know you better."

"It will be my pleasure if you do, Andrew."

"John. Myrna. Thank you for welcoming me back to our home and to Ulster."

John inclined his head. Myrna smiled.

"Doctors, thank you both for your wise and compassionate care. And to Sue and Kitty. Thank you for our conversations. Now, I'm coming to the point. Because of you all, I am having a wonderful Christmas, and I'd like you to understand something. I am not pretending that I am not a sick man.

"But at the moment I am feeling physically very well, and it may come as a surprise, but I truly need you to understand this, that I am not particularly worried about the future. And I am not in what you doctors call denial. I know the facts, but I am at ease with them."

O'Reilly glanced at Barry and was pleased to see his tiny nod of agreement with what O'Reilly had decided was a true statement.

"I have been surrounded by death half my life."

Myrna inhaled sharply and a hand came to her chest and then to her mouth. John sat up straighter. O'Reilly looked at Kitty and met her questioning gaze.

"Gold mining is a dangerous business. I've been going down below to work on my mines for years. Cave-ins and accidents take their toll. One image of Australia is the cuddly koala bear, but the Great South Land has more venomous creatures than any other part of the world. Over the years I've had encounters with at least half a dozen of the one hundred or so poisonous snakes we have in the deserts of Western Australia." He stared at the carpet, then looked up. "I think what I'm trying to say is, we all are going to die, and honestly it does not scare me. My family and Fingal know I was a gambling man in my youth. And mining for gold is like one long game of high stakes whist at White's." He laughed. "But apart from one rather memorable time in 1926—" Andrew looked over to his brother, who smiled broadly and shook his head. "I've faced long odds before—and won. I will not brood on it, and I am going to enjoy whatever time I have left to me to the full. So," he smiled at his host, "in defiance of doctor's orders, Fingal, would you kindly pour me a John Jameson neat?" With that he took his seat again.

O'Reilly grinned and immediately complied. As he poured,

he looked over to Andrew. The man's attitude was one of the most courageous he'd ever seen in all his years in medicine. I've known intense fear under Italian shelling, he thought, and German bombing, but each time it was over quickly. Andrew would be living with this for the rest of his life. He is a brave man.

John was leaning over and shaking his brother's hand.

Kitty said, "Well said, Andrew. Well said."

Myrna stood. "Stand up, brother," and when he did, she folded him in an enormous hug. She had tears in her eyes.

"And that's what I need. Not pity, not sadness, but love and friendship and I have those aplenty."

O'Reilly noticed that Barry and Sue were both smiling, and that Sonny was squeezing Maggie's hand. O'Reilly handed Andrew the drink.

"Thank you." He raised it, saying, "Myrna and John, you'll remember our father's favourite toast?"

Two heads nodded.

"Let's drink to it. Here's to us." He swung the hand holding the drink in a semicircle to include the whole company. "Who's like us? Damn few—and they're all dead. Merry Christmas everyone. Merry Christmas."

Nine voices repeated the toast. Ten glasses went to ten mouths, and when the glasses were lowered, O'Reilly saw nine mouths—and all were smiling. And he was grinning too.

15

A Feast of Fat Things . . . Full of Marrow

"To each one of you I wish a very happy Christmas and if throughout the commonwealth we can all make a sustained effort, perhaps Christmas next year will be a much happier one for many more people."

The black-and-white TV broadcast had begun at three P.M., and like most folks in Ulster, O'Reilly, Kitty, Lars, Kinky, and Archie had been watching. O'Reilly rose, stepped over Arthur Guinness, and switched off the set. The five of them had gathered in the small room on the half-landing reserved strictly for TV watching. He wouldn't have the thing's blank eye staring at him, as he put it, anywhere but in its own special space when he wanted to watch it. "Well, folks," he said, perching on the edge of Kitty's armchair, "what did you think of Her Majesty's Most Gracious Speech from Buckingham Palace?"

"Honestly?" Lars said. "I think the monarchy is a bit of an anachronism, but as long as it's what the majority wants, I'm not complaining."

O'Reilly nodded. "Kinky, what did you think?"

She took her time answering. "Well, sir, Her Majesty is not my queen. I am still an Irish citizen, but very happy here in the wee North. When I was housekeeper here for old Doctor Flanagan, I listened with him when the BBC radio started the tradition in 1932 and King George V read it. I've never missed a year since, except in '36, when King Edward VIII had just abdicated, and in '38 when there simply wasn't one. It's a fine old Christmas tradition, and not only for here. It goes to the whole commonwealth. I think Queen Elizabeth II is a very gracious lady. I thought today's talk about the importance of the family, from one little family to the whole family of man, was very well done, so."

O'Reilly moved back to his chair. "I agree, Kinky, and I can tell you it's given me pause for thought. About families. You here in this room are my family, and that includes Arthur and her ladyship. I have been privileged to add two new members this year, Kitty, my love, and you Archie, and we'll be adding one more, Barry, on January the first. This year I'd like to begin a new tradition. Kinky, ever since I came here in '46, we've watched the King and then the Queen's speech together after I've come home from the marquis's open house. You've served Christmas dinner to me and Lars—and to Ma until she died in '48—and then you've taken yours in your quarters."

"As does be right and proper, sir."

"Well, it doesn't feel right and proper to me any longer. I meant it when I said you're family. Why don't you and Archie join us upstairs for Christmas dinner this year?"

"Oh, Fingal, what a lovely idea. Yes, Kinky, please join us."

Kinky looked at Archie, then at O'Reilly. "Oh, sir, I-I, well, it's a very kind offer, but it wouldn't be right." She took a breath as if she were about to continue, then paused and shook her head. "No, no, it wouldn't be right. But I'll tell you this, sir. When Archie and I have finished our main course, I'll bring in the Christmas pudding and bring two more plates and glasses and join the three of you for dessert and an after-dinner drink, so."

Kinky made a little bob of her head and smiled at Archie, and said, "Yes, we'd be very honoured to do that, sir. Very honoured, so. Now, we'll say no more about it." She rose. "Come on, dear. We've things to do. The turkey soup will be on the table in twenty minutes."

As they left, he heard her say to Archie, "Family. Us. Bless the man."

O'Reilly smiled. "Well, I think Kinky settled that diplomatically. Come on, you two. Upstairs. Our at-home drinks are long gone. Time for a quick pre-prandial." Arthur followed O'Reilly.

"I'll bring her ladyship," Kitty said.

"Seeing it is Christmas Day," O'Reilly said when Kitty and Lars were seated in front of the fireplace where heaped coals glowed and the animals lay close to the brass fender, "I thought this might be in order." He produced an ice bucket containing a bottle of Henkell Trocken. "Archie brought it up from the fridge just before the broadcast."

"How lovely," said Kitty.

The "pop" as he drew the cork made Lady Macbeth sit up and take notice. Arthur, well used to the roar of nearby shotguns, did not stir. Soon three fizzing flutes stood on the sideboard. O'Reilly handed one each to Lars and Kitty and took his own.

Kitty looked at her glass of bubbles. "Fingal, I think that was the loveliest gesture telling Kinky and Archie they are part of our family and inviting them to have their Christmas dinner with us. But I understand how she feels about it not being right. Perhaps she feels the way I felt when I first went to dinner at the big house?"

"Perhaps. But it's true they are our family." He sipped. "I don't know what I would have done without Kinky when I came here in '46. It was Kinky who persuaded me to buy that great lummox over there," he nodded at Arthur, "and he only a wriggling ball of fluff then. Kinky and Arthur were my only Ballybucklebo family. Ma, rest in peace, and Lars were both in Portaferry and in single-handed practice I didn't get much chance to get down there often."

He sipped again. "When Kinky started working for me the master-servant relationship was very clear, but Kinky has been my rock of ages for nearly nineteen years. Times are changing. There's less class distinction now, and so it's easier for me to recognise Kinky not only as my employee, but as a very close friend."

"And in that spirit," Kitty said, "at the time of year that is for families, may I propose the toast, 'To the family of man in general and the family of O'Reilly in particular, of which I am now a member, may it be happy, healthy, and always keep in touch.'"

Three glasses were raised and the toast drunk. All three savoured their wine.

Arthur was probably dreaming of his marrow bone. His eyebrows went up and down like a fiddler's elbow. The tip of his tail twitched.

Perhaps emboldened by her recent triumph over the glass balls, Lady Macbeth put out an exploratory front paw and dabbed at Arthur's tail. O'Reilly didn't hesitate. Setting his glass on the sideboard, he made a grab for her ladyship.

Too late.

Arthur let go an almighty "woof," and a streak of white lightning raced up the tree and in seconds, to the accompaniment of swishing noises and a volley of displaced ornaments rolling on the carpet, Lady Macbeth was perched on a topmost branch.

When all three eventually stopped laughing, O'Reilly said,

"I think she looks like one of the gargoyles on Notre-Dame Cathedral in Paris," and set them off again.

It took some "push-wushing," and arm-stretching on O'Reilly's part to prise her loose and as he did, Kinky's voice came up the stairs. "I'm serving the soup in two minutes."

"Right," said O'Reilly. "Kitty, please bring my glass. Lars, the bubbles, and you, your ladyship, I'm taking to the kitchen, and I'll have to think about that ham and turkey I promised you this morning." Arthur, O'Reilly thought, can sleep on.

The turkey soup had, as always, been delicious. O'Reilly at the head of the table poured wine for Kitty seated to his right and Lars to his left.

The table was covered with a white Irish linen tablecloth and adorned with a small holly wreath surrounded by two tall candles in silver candlesticks. The diners' napkins were scarlet.

Kinky appeared. "All done?"

Kitty said, "I must get that recipe, Kinky, it was fantastic."

"Thank you. And so, you shall." She put the used plates on the tray. "We'll be back soon with the main course."

"Now," said O'Reilly, "a trip down memory lane." He picked up a red and gold paper tube a foot in length and crimped at either end. "Kitty." He grasped one end and offered her the other. "Ready?"

She nodded.

"Pull." Both tugged. The thing tore apart with a loud crack and a smell of burnt gunpowder.

Kitty had the longer bit and dumped out a small red plastic E-type Jaguar car and a bright blue roll of paper, which she unfurled to transform into a paper crown. She placed it on her head of shiny black hair at a jaunty angle. What was left was a small piece of white paper. "When is a door not a door?" she read.

O'Reilly remembered asking that question of Lars when they lived in Holywood as children. He feigned ignorance as clearly did Lars.

Kitty turned the strip over. "When it's ajar." She groaned. "That is terrible."

"Not when you're six," Lars said.

"True," said Kitty.

By the time two more Christmas crackers had been torn apart and the riddles asked and answered, Lars wore a green paper crown and O'Reilly a gold one, the bubbly was finished, and O'Reilly had opened a bottle of Entre-Deux-Mers. Kinky and Archie came in with loaded trays accompanied by the aroma of roast turkey.

Kinky said, "You'll carve on the sideboard as usual, sir?"

"I will, thanks. Will you pour the wine please, Lars?" O'Reilly lifted the carving knife and steel and, with swift, well-practised strokes, put an edge on the knife that would slice paper.

Kinky meanwhile had set the steaming turkey, its skin a rich golden brown, on the sideboard. It was surrounded by small chipolatas. She pointed at the neck end, "Chestnut stuffing," and at the vent end, "sausage meat stuffing." Next came the cold glazed ham, its glistening surface scored into small diamonds, each of which was pierced by a single clove.

As O'Reilly began to carve the ham, Archie was putting down and naming dishes on the tablecloth. "Mashed potatoes, roast potatoes, Brussels sprouts, bread sauce, and turkey gravy."

O'Reilly handed Kinky a loaded plate. "Now, Kinky, after

all these years I know what you like, so I've ham and turkey, chestnut stuffing and chipolatas on your plate, so help yourself to spuds, bread sauce, sprouts, and gravy, but Archie?"

"A little ham and some dark turkey, please, sir. And some of both stuffings, but I'm not so keen on those little cocktail sausages."

Kinky sniffed at that, as if to say, not yet, but wait until you try mine cold when you and I are having leftovers from this feast at your house tomorrow.

The plate was filled in no time and handed over and Kinky and Archie added their portions of side dishes.

O'Reilly said, "Before you go on behalf of Kitty, Lars, and me, a thousand thanks to you both for all your hard work."

"Hear him," Lars said.

Kitty raised her glass.

Kinky smiled her thanks and inclined her head, and as she and Archie headed for the door to complete their dinner in Kinky's quarters, O'Reilly said, "Don't forget there's a bottle of wine in the fridge and if you want seconds come right back here."

Archie said, "We certainly will."

"And we'll be back with the pudding soon," Kinky said as they took their leave.

O'Reilly had not been idle. Slices of turkey and ham lay on their respective plates. He knew Lars's tastes, and anyway ladies first. He said to Kitty, "And you, my love?"

Kitty was looking amazed at the extent of the spread. "Small helpings, small or our family alone will keep Alice Moloney busy for all of January. White and dark meat, both stuffings, and chipolatas, please. I may come back for ham if I've got room."

In short order all three plates were full, all three glasses charged. O'Reilly looked at his loaded plate. He inhaled the competing scents, felt his mouth water, and raised his glass. "I was very impressed by how Andrew behaved this morning. There is one very brave man, and I liked the way he used their father's favourite toast taken from the Lowland Scots. Our father's was too, so please join me and Lars, Kitty, and remember it for next year."

They raised their glasses.

"Some hae meat and cannae eat,
"And some wad eat that want it,
"But we hae meat and we can eat
"So, let the Lord be thankit."

Kitty echoed, "So let the Lord be thankit."

They drank, and then in anticipatory silence everybody began to eat.

The table had been cleared, and dessert dishes and a dish of brandy butter set on the cloth by O'Reilly. He, now full of the Christmas spirit, had asked Kinky to give Lady Macbeth a few scraps of turkey and ham before returning both to the pantry. Arthur would get his treats on his way to his bed and his marrow bone later tonight.

Archie set the Christmas pudding, dark brown, studded with raisins, and topped with a holly sprig, near O'Reilly. Kinky poured nearly boiling brandy from a saucepan over the pudding and O'Reilly dropped a lit match onto the plate. The brandy fumes were ignited with a small "whoof," and blue flames danced over the plate and the pudding, crisping the holly sprig at its edges.

As he waited for the flames to subside, O'Reilly asked Archie to sit by Kitty. "And Kinky," he said, "why don't you take off your apron. You and Archie are our guests, and you are off duty."

She smiled, did as she had been asked, folded it, set it on a vacant chair, and sat beside Lars.

The flames guttered out and O'Reilly served everybody, then rose and picked up the ice bucket. "For those who prefer a dry white, I'll ask Lars to do the honours. But you, Kinky, know probably better than anyone that I have a sweet tooth. I'm going to enjoy a glass of Sauternes with my dessert. Would anyone care to join me?"

Kinky said, "Yes, please, sir."

He moved to her place. "I think today, old friend, we can drop the 'sir.'"

Kinky blushed but grinned widely. "Thank you for that and for the wine. It has been a great privilege to have served in this house and to have that service respected and valued, so. And it will be a pleasure to go on serving part-time after Archie and I have exchanged our vows in April."

Kitty said, "Well said, Kinky, and it's been a great relief to know you will be staying on."

O'Reilly thought, I believe that's the longest speech I've ever heard Kinky make. I wonder if she prepared it in advance. "Bravo, Kinky. Now, I'm falling down on my duties as host." He retook his seat and began serving portions of Christmas pudding. He passed one down to Kinky. "Lars, please pass Kinky the brandy butter."

Archie was served next. "Thank you, Doctor, and like Kinky, may I tell you how proud we are to have been invited, so we are." He helped himself to brandy butter and passed it to Kitty. "Here you are, Mrs. O'Reilly."

"Thank you."

O'Reilly had finished serving everyone but himself, and as he placed his portion on his dessert dish, he noticed that Kinky was swaying, her eyes were glazed, her breathing shallow and rapid. He got to his feet. What in the name of the wee man—?

He had just reached her chair when her eyes opened wide, she stopped swaying, and her gaze held his. She spoke slowly. "I saw it again. Some wrong to be done to little Jill Driscoll tomorrow. She's lost her faith in something important." She nodded to herself and her face was clouded.

"Lost her faith in what?" said O'Reilly.

"I-I don't know. I can feel her fear and disappointment. But not the reason. Wait—the sweep—"

O'Reilly's eyes widened. "The sweep?"

"I see the chimney sweep, Mister Gilligan, on a cottage roof."

O'Reilly's eyes widened and he smiled. Kinky might not know the wrong to be done to Jill Driscoll tomorrow but he was quite sure he did. And he also knew how it could be righted.

16

A Letter to My Love

"Eat up however little much is in it," said Kinky on Boxing Day as she served up a rashers-and-eggs breakfast to O'Reilly, Kitty, and Lars. "Now, sir, I'm leaving a small bowl of Frank Cooper's Oxford marmalade because I know you prefer it, and my own Seville orange marmalade for Mister Lars and Mrs. O'Reilly. And there's two pots for you to take home to Portaferry, sir."

"Thank you, Kinky," Lars said.

"I hope it doesn't put your housekeeper's nose out of joint," Kinky said with a sniff, "but I know you favour mine over hers, so."

"I do, Kinky. That's very kind. She will just have to thole it as best she can."

"I'm off now. Archie's picking me up in the milk-float."

O'Reilly was glad his housekeeper was getting a well-deserved day off at Archie's house. They would have a belated celebration with Archie's sergeant son, Rory, who was stationed at Place Barracks in Holywood and had been on duty yesterday.

"Don't you forget, sir, to have a wee word with Mister Gilligan, the sweep."

"I'll not, Kinky. Not after what you told me yesterday about Jill Driscoll. In fact, I've already called him."

So, the festivities were over for another year, thought O'Reilly as he shrugged into his heavy overcoat and made his way to the Rover. After breakfast, Kitty had headed to the hospital, Lars to Portaferry, Barry had the day off, and O'Reilly was on call. Praise be there'd been none so O'Reilly had finished *The Caine Mutiny* and now, at eleven, was heading to the housing estate with Arthur Guinness in the backseat, to see the chimney sweep. The Contractors Bureau would pick up the phone and he'd check in with them on his return. He'd not be long.

As he knocked on Mister Gilligan's door, the snow began to fall. The door opened on a man in his mid-fifties with a short-back-and-sides cut of his ginger hair, blue eyes, and deep laugh lines at their corners.

"Come on in out of that, Doctor."

The snow was falling heavily now.

"Thank you. I'll only take a minute or two."

He was shown into a neat parlour and offered a chair. "I heard you're going to sweep the Driscolls' chimney today?"

"Why, I am, sir. At noon. How did you come to know that?" The man leaned forward and peered at O'Reilly. "Is something wrong?"

O'Reilly ignored the man's questions. "I remember hearing some discreet talk in the pub about how last Christmas Eve you restored a little girl's faith in Santa Claus."

"Och, aye. I did. Made my Christmas, so it did."

"I fear you may need to do it again today, so in case you don't have any I brought you these." He passed something into the sweep's callused hand.

He glanced, then shoved them into his overall pocket with a grin. "A wink's as good as a nod to a blind horse. If I need to,

I'll see her right." He cocked his head to one side. "Did Mrs. Kincaid tell you about this?"

"She did."

The sweep winked. "Don't worry. I'll take care of the wee girl."

"Thank you. Now, one last question. How long after you get there will you be ready to climb up on the roof?"

The sweep frowned, ticked off steps on his fingers. "Let's see. I've to unpack my stuff, get it all into the house, spread a big canvas sheet in front of the fireplace, then get my brush—"

O'Reilly chuckled. "No more geese up the chimney. Or little boys." He remembered as a child reading Charles Kingsley's *The Water Babies* about a boy sweep. The little book had been one of the forces driving Parliament to outlaw the practice in 1875.

Mister Gilligan answered, somewhat curtly, "No, sir. My brush has a long bamboo shaft and I push it up until I reckon the brush is ready til come out at the top. That's when I need til get up on the roof. The whole business'll take half an hour."

"Good. Thank you. That's all I need to know. I'll be waiting outside their cottage."

"Suit yourself, Doc. But I won't fail you nor the wee girl."

O'Reilly rose. "Thank you, Mister Gilligan. I've every faith in you. Now, I'll see myself out."

As he drove off, he spoke to Arthur, a habit he'd developed in the forties when feeling lonely. "I've been racking my brains for an excuse to be there. There's no medical reason for me to drop in, but it's a lovely walk round the beach there and you and I, sir, are going to walk it."

What Arthur made of the explanation O'Reilly had no idea,

but the word "walk," spoken twice, made the Lab prick up his ears and start making little grumbling noises in his throat.

O'Reilly approached the Driscolls' cottage, with Arthur leading the way snapping at falling snowflakes. Parked outside were Declan Driscoll's green Morris Minor and Mister Gilligan's van.

The timing was perfect. The front door opened and out came Mister Gilligan followed by Jill and a small boy. O'Reilly recognized eight-year-old John Robinson, son of a shipyard riveter and his wife, who worked part-time in Phyllis Cadogan's tobacconist's. The children, bundled against the cold, were deep in conversation.

O'Reilly remembered being fascinated by sweeps when he was a child. It seemed modern children were no less intrigued.

"Hello, Doctor," the sweep said wryly. "Walking Arthur then, are you?"

"Hello, Doctor O'Reilly," said John. "Mrs. Driscoll said it was all right to come out by ourselves and help Mister Gilligan."

Jill's voice was trembly when she said, "John thinks Santa doesn't come down the chimney, Doctor, especially a sooty one like ours that needed sweeping."

"I think he comes in through the front door," said the boy. "I don't see how he could get reindeer, and a sleigh, on that little roof. And he must get dead dirty."

Jill hiccuped a sigh. "I suppose, but my daddy says he does, so, and that's why I hang my stocking on the mantel and leave biccies and eggnog for him."

O'Reilly sighed. So, this was how it started, the shaking of her belief in Santa, a belief O'Reilly, just four days ago, had made come true. Why couldn't little Jilly Driscoll, who had had her world shaken by the separation of her mother and father, keep her faith in the jolly old elf for another year or so?

O'Reilly thought John was going to continue the debate, but the lad must have had enough wit to let the hare sit.

Mister Gilligan said, "It's getting cold out here and I've to get up on that there roof. Are you two going to keep blethering on or are you going to help me?"

Jill said, "Sorry, Mister Gilligan. We'll help."

He lifted a ladder from where he had left it and propped it against the eaves' trough. He pointed up. "See that wire mesh cone over the chimney? It's to stop birds nesting. I need to swing it out of the way, then come down and go in and push my brush til it comes right out. When that happens I want my helpers to come in and tell me. All right?"

O'Reilly had been watching the expressions on the children's faces, John still stubborn, clearly convinced he was right, Jill puzzled and confused about Santa.

The sweep said, "Now I'm off."

In moments he had reached the chimney, and opened it up. As he climbed down through the falling snow, O'Reilly said to John, "You still don't believe Santa can get on the roof?"

The boy shook his head.

Jill looked close to tears. "P'rhaps—p'rhaps Santa does use the door."

"Well, if he does," Mister Gilligan held his closed right fist in front of Jill, and winked at O'Reilly, "can somebody explain to me why I found these?" He opened his hand and gave the wee girl two silver sleigh bells. "They were settin' there, just beside the chimney."

John's eyes opened wide and he smiled. Jill laughed, shook the bells, and in her face was all the unbound joy of every child at Christmas.

O'Reilly late-lunched well on cold leftovers with the sound of those silver sleigh bells still jingling in his ears. He had checked in with the Bureau as soon as he got back to Number One, but there had been no calls to disturb his meal of a turkey drumstick, stuffing, bread sauce, slices of ham, chipolatas, and cold Christmas pudding with brandy butter for dessert. While his inner man was very satisfied, outside the weather was appalling, the light practically nonexistent. The crystal chandelier over the table glowed in the half-light.

Both animals, her ladyship's momentary lack of self-control clearly forgiven by Arthur, were in the upstairs lounge in front of the fire where he joined them. He collapsed gratefully into his armchair, and promptly fell asleep.

He woke up with a start, blinked, knuckled his eyes, shook his head. Good Lord. Quarter to four. He stood up cautiously, still disoriented from the deep sleep, and crossed the floor to look out the bow window now half-blocked with snow.

A strong north wind had blown up and the snowfall was much heavier. He could see drifts piling up against the low wall at the front of Number One, and the Bangor to Belfast Road was covered and there were no tyre tracks. He wondered if the road were closed on both sides of Ballybucklebo. He hoped no one was going to need medical attention. And how was Kitty going to manage? She'd be off duty at four. Surely to God she wouldn't try to drive home in that lot?

The double ring of the upstairs telephone had him rushing to grab the receiver. A patient?

"Hello? O'Reilly."

"Fingal?"

It was Kitty. He felt his pulse rate slow down.

"Yes, pet."

"I'm so glad you're home. Have you had a good afternoon?"

"Yes, and I just woke up from a nap. I was out earlier at the Driscolls. Kinky was right. I'll tell you all about it when you get home."

"That's why I'm ringing. It doesn't look like I'm going to make it. We've been told both the roads and the railway from Belfast to Ballybucklebo are blocked and no one can be sure when they'll open again. I'll be staying here in the nurses' quarters. Half the student nurses are still on holiday. There's lots of room." She paused. "I'm sorry, Fingal. I know you'd hoped I'd stay home on Boxing Day but I like to let my nurses with children have the day off."

Damn. He pursed his lips and told himself what can't be cured must be endured. "I'm sorry too. We've had such a lovely Christmas. I was looking forward to our evening, but as long as you'll be all right—"

"Of course I will. The cafeteria even has some turkey. But save me some leftovers for tomorrow." She laughed and O'Reilly could tell she was fine.

The lights in the lounge flickered, then burned brightly again. "We've just had a threatened power cut. It must be brutal outside. I'm glad you won't be driving."

"You know where the candles are, Fingal?"

"I do. The fire's lit here upstairs and—"

The lights flicked again, recovered, but the phone went dead.

He rattled the receiver rest. "Hello. Hello."

Dead. "Damn and blast." He put the receiver back on its cradle. At least he knew Kitty wasn't out in it and had somewhere to sleep tonight.

He went back downstairs and through to the kitchen to the cupboard where Kinky kept emergency supplies. He fixed candles into two holders and brought two spare candles as well. The matches he used to light his pipe were in his trouser pocket.

He walked back along the hall, bitterly disappointed he'd not be seeing Kitty tonight. As he drew level with the surgery he remembered that ever since she'd given him his old love letters he'd been working his way through them. And there was one left.

O'Reilly returned to the upstairs lounge, greeted Arthur and Lady Macbeth, and put another shovelful of coal on the fire. He went to close the curtains and saw that the blizzard had not abated.

He put the candles on the mantelpiece, just in case, and returned to his comfortable armchair in front of the fire.

The envelope he was carrying was dated January 15, 1965, a Saturday—and it had snowed then too. Rather like tonight, Kitty had been going to come down, but the roads were closed. So instead of seeing her he had written his feelings down in a letter.

Dearest Kitty,

The snow started in the early hours of this morning, great tumbling flakes reflecting the dim streetlights.

Later in the morning I stood and watched it blanket the

road, the grounds and steeple of the Presbyterian Church until, with a rending crash, a yew branch, bowed under its burden of snow, fell to the ground.

I'm now sitting upstairs, having just finished reading one of your old letters, your gossamer thread of attachment to me. Your picture is on the mantel, and I'm longing to have you here but am content to hear your voice in the words on the page and talk to you through this letter.

Outside the snow falls and falls, covering my world and I, cocooned within my house, listen to the almost silence. In the murmuring of the falling flakes I think I hear your voice whisper, "Darling, I love you."

The snow has fallen so deeply that had you been here we would be snowed in alone. We would have sat in this room, the fire roaring, music of your choice on the gramophone. We would be warm in the red glow of the fire, cut off from the whole world and anything in it that could harm us. Snug and snuggled in our nest and our love, so deep, so true, we would need no words as we held each other and fell asleep in front of the fire while outside the winter raged.

But I am alone. How dare the snow fall? How dare it lie in such coruscating beauty, sparkling in the rays of the now visible sun and paralyzing our world so cars cannot run?

The snow dares to fall because it is inanimate, unthinking. It doesn't care if it disrupts the petty lives of men with its pristine loveliness. It is a force unto itself, wild, uncontrollable.

The way I love you is wild and uncontrollable, but my love is not unthinking. It is a living, growing, animate being that is deeper than the drifts outside my window. My love defies all logic. Without it there would be no joy, no beauty.

I lost you once and searched for you, but I never found you. I needn't have looked so hard. You found me and enveloped me in your love, just as the snowstorm has covered Ballybucklebo.

In a few days the snow will have gone, and its disruptiveness, and its beauty, will be forgotten.

My love for you will not melt like the snow. My love for you is not the false icing of the snow that presently caps the church steeple. It is as solid and enduring as the church itself.

Kitty, Kitty, Kitty, I love you

O'Reilly sat back, his right arm dangling over the arm of the chair, letter grasped loosely between thumb and forefinger. There was a lump in his throat, but he felt so secure in that love that his eyes were dry. She would be home tomorrow evening.

Tonight, he was on his own, and although Boxing Day was almost over, he wanted to keep the season alive. He stood, opened the gramophone, and selected Frank Sinatra's "Have Yourself a Merry Little Christmas." O'Reilly smiled as the violin and harp began, followed by that sublime voice, like an old friend's confiding tones.

And hadn't the O'Reillys had a merry one this year, their first together as man and wife? Andrew MacNeill was reconciled with his sister, Myrna, and at ease with his illness; Barry Laverty back to the practice and about to be a partner; Kinky and Archie more closely drawn into the O'Reilly family after a magnificent Christmas dinner. And little Jill Driscoll's family was reunited and her joy in Santa restored with the help of Kinky's sight and a chimney sweep.

Ol' Blue Eyes sang the last line of "Merry Little Christmas" and the player switched itself off.

"And do you know?" O'Reilly addressed the animals, both of whom stared at him, "Mister Francis Albert Sinatra is only half-right. The O'Reillys did have themselves a merry Christmas—but there was nothing little about it. It was love, it was happiness, it was a reminder of what the season really means, and it certainly wasn't little—for us it was enormous."

Afterword

Hello again. It's me, Mrs. Maureen Kincaid, née O'Hanlon, familiarly called Kinky. When your man Patrick Taylor's first book was going to come out, Doctor O'Reilly started it all when he suggested that I should put in some Irish recipes. I've been at that now every time a new book is finished.

It's two weeks since Christmas and things in Ballybucklebo and at Number One Main Street are back to normal. That nice Driscoll family went back to County Cork on New Year's Day. His lordship's brother, Mister Andrew MacNeill, him that was here for the O'Reilly's at-home on Christmas Day, left to go back to Australia yesterday, but I hear he has plans to visit here in a few years. And with Doctor Laverty now a partner, Doctor O'Reilly is not so run off his feet. Neither am I but it won't be long until I'll be going round like a bee on a hot brick getting things ready for when Archie and I get married in April.

And I have a chance this morning to put pen to paper and let you have some more. This time I'm doing:

Winter Vegetable Soup, Salmon with Parmesan Topping, Lemon Fridge Cake, and Seville Orange Marmalade as dishes that can be enjoyed year-round, one special Christmas finger food, and a typical Irish dinner main course to be eaten on Christmas Eve.

I hope you will try them and enjoy them.

Maureen Kincaid

Year-Round Dishes

Winter Vegetable Soup

1 tablespoon of sunflower or canola oil
1 large potato, peeled and chopped
2 onions, chopped
2 carrots, peeled and chopped
1 stick celery, chopped
2 fat leeks, washed and chopped
1 garlic clove, chopped
1 cup lentils, washed
1 cup dried peas, soaked overnight and washed thoroughly
40 oz. / 1.2 L. vegetable or chicken stock (cubes or powder are fine)
20 oz. / 590 mL. water
Small bunch of parsley, chopped
Salt and freshly ground black pepper to taste

Heat the oil gently in a large saucepan and add the chopped vegetables gradually.

Cover with a sheet of parchment paper and let the vegetables sweat over a gentle heat for 10 minutes. Remove the parchment paper and add the garlic, lentils, peas, and stock. Bring to the boil, cover with a lid, and simmer gently for about an hour. Add the water, and you may need to add more if the soup is too thick.

Finally add the chopped parsley and salt and freshly ground black pepper to taste.

Kinky's Note: You could a use a ham bone instead of stock cubes.

Salmon with Parmesan Topping

1 salmon fillet per serving of about 5–6 oz. / 150–175 g.

Topping for 6 fillets
6 oz. / 150 g. cream cheese
2 tablespoons of chopped dill
1 clove of garlic, crushed
Grated rind of 1 small lemon
1 teaspoon lemon juice
1 oz. / 25 g. of white breadcrumbs or panko
1 oz. / 25 g. Parmesan cheese, grated
Salt and freshly ground black pepper

Preheat the oven to 400°F / 200°C.

Dry the fillets with a kitchen roll then season with salt and pepper on both sides and lay on greased parchment paper on a baking tray.

Mix the cream cheese with chopped dill, garlic, lemon rind, and juice. If you warm this for a few seconds in the microwave it will be easier to spread.

Spread this on top of each fillet.

Mix together the crumbs and Parmesan and spread this on top of the cream cheese mixture and finish with a grind of black pepper.

Bake in the oven for 15 to 20 minutes until done. Allow to rest for 3 minutes before serving with garden peas or asparagus.

Lemon Fridge Cake

This is a very quick, light dessert that is easy to prepare in advance and freezes very well.

The cake
6 oz. / 170 g. butter, softened
6 oz. / 170 g. sugar
3 eggs at room temperature
6 oz. / 170 g. flour
2 teaspoons baking powder
½ teaspoon salt

The lemon layers
3½ oz. / 100 g. butter, softened
3½ oz. / 100 g. sugar
3 large eggs, separated
Grated rind and juice of 1 lemon

To finish
8 oz. / 235 mL. heavy cream, whipped
Raspberries

Make the cake first.

Preheat the oven to 325°F / 170°C. Grease and line with parchment paper 2 rectangular loaf-size baking tins, 9 by 5 inch / 23 by 12 cm.

Using an electric mixer, beat the butter, sugar, and eggs in a large bowl for a minute or so. Sift the flour and baking powder with the salt into the bowl and fold in. This should be a soft dropping consistency. If it is not, just add a little milk and beat it some more.

Now divide the mixture between the two tins, smooth the tops, and bake for 30 to 35 minutes.

To tell if they are ready, lightly touch the center with your finger. If it leaves no impression and the cake springs back, they are done.

Cool the cakes on a rack.

THE LEMON LAYERS

Beat the butter and sugar until light and fluffy. Then add the egg yolks, lemon rind, and juice.

Don't worry if it looks curdled. In a separate bowl beat the egg whites until stiff and fold into the lemon mixture.

By now the cakes will have cooled down. Slice each cake along the length twice to give 3 pieces.

Spread the lemon mixture along each top and sandwich together. Then spread the lemon mixture over the top. Put each cake back in the baking tin, lifting with the parchment paper. Wait a few hours or overnight before using or freezing to let the lemon mix soak into the cake.

To finish, cover the top and sides with whipped cream and put raspberries on top.

Kinky's note: To save time you could use trifle sponges, or a store-bought plain cake such as a Madeira or an angel cake.

SEVILLE ORANGE MARMALADE

2 lbs 3 oz. / 1 kg. Seville oranges
1 large lemon

Enough water to cover the fruit
Around 4 lbs. 6 oz. / 2 kg. sugar
A knob of butter

I like to make my marmalade over a period of 2 days.

Start by cutting the oranges and lemon in half. Squeeze the juice from each half into a very large heavy-bottomed saucepan. An electric citrus squeezer is handy for this. Collect the pith and pips that stick to the squeezer and put them in a small jug and set to one side. These contain most of the pectin, which will help the marmalade to set.

Cut the now empty fruit halves into shreds as thick or as fine as you like and put them in the pan with the juice and add enough water to cover the fruit and simmer gently over a low heat for 2 hours, stirring occasionally.

Pour boiling water over the pith and pips in the jug and leave overnight.

Next day pour the contents of the jug through a strainer into the pan. You will notice how gelatinous this looks and it will really help the marmalade to set.

Put your clean, washed jars into the oven to sterilise them at a temperature of 250°F or 130°C for about 20 minutes.

Bring the pan to a boil and add the sugar gradually to the fruit, stirring until it has dissolved.

Keep the pan at a high heat and a rolling boil and continue to stir regularly to make sure it does not burn. You may notice a white scum form at the top so just add a knob of butter and it will disappear by the time you are ready to pot it.

After about 20 minutes start testing for a set. Just bring some up on your wooden spoon, allow it to cool slightly, and turn the spoon sideways. If some of the mixture drops cling to the edge of the spoon the marmalade is ready. One other method is to chill a plate in the fridge and put a spoonful on it. Put the plate back in the fridge and check it in a few minutes by pushing your finger on it. If it wrinkles you have reached setting point.

Allow to cool for about 20 minutes before giving one final stir. Use a jug to pour the marmalade into the jars.

Kinky's note: An alternative way of calculating the amount of sugar necessary is to measure the amount of liquid in the pan and add 1 lb. / 450 g. sugar to every 20 oz. / 590 mL. of orange liquid.

I use a wooden spoon as a dipstick on which I have previously marked the measurements.

Finger Food

One favourite of Doctor O'Reilly's is gravadlax on wheaten bread. Here are the recipes for both.

Irish Wheaten Bread*

10 oz. / 284 g. all-purpose flour
10 oz. / 284 g. whole-wheat flour
6 oz. / 170 g. old-fashioned rolled oats
2 oz. / 56 g. sunflower seeds or pumpkin seeds
2 tablespoons sugar
1 tablespoon salt
2 tablespoons canola or sunflower oil, or you can use butter

* This is also known as Irish soda bread or brown bread.

1 tablespoon bicarbonate of soda (baking soda)
1 teaspoon of cream of tartar
1 L / 34 fluid oz. buttermilk or slightly less

Preheat the oven to 400°F / 200°C.

Grease two 9-by-5-inch (23x12cm) loaf tins well, line them with greased parchment. Mix all the dry ingredients in a large bowl. If you are using butter you will need to rub it in with your fingertips. (If you are using oil, add it to the buttermilk.) Dissolve the bicarbonate of soda and the cream of tartar in a cup of buttermilk. This will froth up so be careful to pour it into the flour mixture soon after. Now make a well in the centre of the dry ingredients and add the buttermilk and oil (if using). You add the remaining milk gradually because sometimes you may need to add more or less depending on the brand of flour used or even the weather conditions. However, what you are aiming for is a nice soft dropping consistency.

Divide the mixture between the two loaf tins. Make an indent down the centre of the dough with the blade of a knife. Bake in the oven at 400°F / 200°C for 15 minutes, then turn the oven down to 350°F / 180°C and bake for a further 35 to 45 minutes. Turn the bread out onto the rack to cool. If it is ready it will sound hollow when the bottom is tapped. Leave to cool covered with a damp teacloth.

You can make variations by adding or substituting various ingredients. I sometimes add more whole wheat flour than plain flour or different seeds. Adding treacle or molasses gives a rich brown colour. I even add crushed garlic if I'm planning to use the bread as an accompaniment with soup or a savoury starter.

Ma never weighed her ingredients. Like a lot of Irish cooks she just used handfuls and instinctively knew when it was right.

Kinky's Note: If you are using treacle or molasses, measure it with the same spoon that you used for the oil and it will slide off easily.

I like to serve my smoked salmon on my wheaten bread with a squeeze of lemon, freshly ground black pepper, and a few sprigs of parsley for decoration. I think my own home-cured gravadlax makes this dish very special. Sure it takes no time at all.

Use Atlantic salmon if you can get it, for isn't that the fish we eat in Ireland?

Gravadlax, Irish-Style

1 centre-cut salmon fillet weighing about 450 g. / 1 lb. with the bones removed. Leave the skin on, if there is any, as it will help when you are going to slice it.
Juice of 2 limes or lemons
1 tablespoon sea salt
1 tablespoon sugar
A good bunch of dill

Cut salmon into 2 pieces and lay one half, skin side down, in a deep dish, or a loaf tin, lined with cling film.

Mix the juice, salt, and sugar together. Reserve some of the dill for a garnish and chop the rest of the washed dill finely. Spread half of it over the fish in the dish. Place the rest of the fish on top, skin side up, and cover with the remaining dill. Pour the juice mixture over the salmon. Bring the sides of the cling film over the top to seal it. Now place a weight on top of the cling wrap. Just whatever you have handy, such as a couple of tins of baked beans or anything else that feels just as heavy, would do. Place in the fridge and leave for a total time of 24 to 36 hours. The fish "cooks" or "cures" in the sweet acidic juice. I think it helps if you remove the weights and turn it over once, then replace the weights and leave to finish curing.

Remove from the fridge and rinse both pieces of salmon in ice-cold water to wash off most of the dill. Then pat it dry between sheets of kitchen paper.

Place the fish on a cutting board and slice into very thin slices, removing it from the skin as you cut. A very sharp knife is required.

Arrange on a plate decorated with thin slices of cucumber, dill fronds, capers, and lemon wedges.

Serve buttered Irish wheaten bread and freshly ground pepper to accompany.

Christmas Eve Dinner Main Course

Roast Duck Breasts

2 duck breasts—skin on

Preheat the oven to 425°F / 200°C.

Dry each breast with a paper towel and remove the tendon.

With a sharp knife make a crisscross diamond pattern on the skin.

Place the breasts skin side down into a deep, cold frying pan. Do not add any butter or oil.

Turn up the heat and cook until the skin becomes quite crispy and the fat has been released.

Pour off the fat and save for roasting potatoes.

Turn the breasts over so that the crispy skin is on top. Now you can either transfer them to a roasting tin or, if your pan is ovenproof, place the pan in the oven for 5 to 8 minutes for medium and a few minutes more for well-done.

Allow to rest for 5 minutes before slicing each one diagonally against the grain.

Sage and Onion Stuffing

I like to use Mrs. Beeton's* recipe for this stuffing, which she recommended for use with duck, geese, or pork. The cost of this was 4 pence.

Here it is:

4 large onions
10 sage leaves
4 oz. / 113 g. breadcrumbs
1½ oz. / 40 g. butter
1 egg yolk
Salt and pepper to taste

Peel the onions and put them in boiling water and let them simmer for 5 minutes or rather longer, and just before they are taken out put in the sage leaves to take off their rawness. Chop both of these very fine, add the bread, seasonings, and butter, and work the whole together with the yolk of an egg, when the stuffing will be ready for use.

* From *The Book of Household Management* by Mrs. Isabella Beeton, first published in 1861.

Roast Parsnips

500 g. / 1 lb. 2 oz. parsnips, peeled and cut into quarters lengthways
4 tablespoons sherry
4 tablespoons clear honey
Salt and freshly ground pepper

Preheat the oven to 400°F / 200°C

Place the parsnips, sherry, and honey into a baking tray and mix to coat the parsnips. Season with salt and freshly ground black pepper.

Roast in the oven for 30 minutes, turning halfway through, until the parsnips are tender and golden brown.

Roast Potatoes

1 or 2 potatoes per person
2 tablespoons duck fat or canola oil
Pinch sea salt
1 teaspoon thyme leaves

Preheat the oven to 400°F / 200°C.

Simmer the potatoes in a large pan of salted boiling water for 4 to 5 minutes, or until the outside of the potatoes are beginning to soften.

Thoroughly drain the potatoes and dry for a minute or so. Now give them a good shake around in the pan to roughen up the edges.

Melt the duck fat or heat the oil in a deep flameproof roasting tray on a high heat and fry the potatoes on each side until they begin to brown.

Sprinkle with salt, to taste, and roast for 30 minutes, or until starting to colour.

Turn the potatoes and return to the oven for a further 20 to 30 minutes, or until golden brown and crisp. Sprinkle with thyme before serving.

So, there it is. I hope you will try these and enjoy them all. I'm beginning to think that at the rate this fellow Taylor keeps churning out these stories, I'll have put so many of my recipes at the end of his books I'll have collected up enough to put in my own cookbook.

MRS. MAUREEN "KINKY" KINCAID
Housekeeper to Doctor Fingal O'Reilly
One Main Street
Ballybucklebo
County Down
Northern Ireland

Glossary

I have in all the previous Irish Country novels provided a glossary to help the reader who is unfamiliar with the vagaries of the Queen's English as it may be spoken by the majority of people in Ulster. This is a regional dialect akin to English as spoken in Yorkshire or on Tyneside. It is not Ulster-Scots, which is claimed to be a distinct language in its own right. I confess I am not a speaker.

Today in Ulster (but not 1965 when this book is set) official signs are written in English, Irish, and Ulster-Scots. The washroom sign would read Toilets, *Leithris* (Irish), and *Cludgies* (Ulster-Scots). I hope what follows here will enhance your enjoyment of the work, although, I am afraid, it will not improve your command of Ulster-Scots.

***a chara*:** Irish. My dear.

away off and (feel your head/bumps/chase yourself): Don't be stupid.

ball (of teal): Ulster collective noun for a small flock of ducks.

Barbour: A clothing company famous for its outdoor wear much favoured by the huntin', shootin', fishin' folks.

BBC: British Broadcasting Corporation. State-run commercial-free TV and radio.

blethering on: Talking incessantly usually about trivia.

bollix (unmitigated): Testicle (complete). Not a term of endearment.

Bonnaught: Irish mercenary of the fourteenth century.

boot: Of a car. Trunk.
both legs the same length: Standing about idly.
bounce: Of a cheque. Not be honoured by the bank. Returned NSF (Not Sufficient Funds).
brave: Very large.
break up: School. Close for holidays.
Brent geese: Brant geese.
burp: Belch.
chapel: Not an architectural term. In Ulster, Protestant places of worship were churches. Catholic ones, chapels.
cheap at half the price: A strange way of saying an item is not very expensive.
come on on (on) in: Is not a typographical error. This item of Ulsterspeak drives spellcheck mad.
dingo: Australian wild dog.
divinity classes: Christian religious instruction given in school.
double negative, can't feel nothing: Can't feel anything.
fair play to you: You are doing the right thing.
fender: A low barrier, usually brass, set to surround the tiles in front of a grate to prevent any ember which might fall out from burning the carpet.
fishmonger: Seller of seafood.
foundered: Frozen stiff.
good man ma Da: Literally good man my father but is a high level of praise.
hang about: Hold on. Wait a minute.
hokey (by the): Expression of surprise.
hoover (to): vacuum (to).
I'm your man: You can count on me.

laugh like a drain: Laugh uncontrollably.

legless: Drunk.

let the hare sit: Let sleeping dogs lie.

lift: Elevator.

liltie: Irish whirling dervish.

lorry: Truck.

marzipan: Almond paste.

milk float: A small electrically powered vehicle with a cab and an open flatbed used by milkmen to make home deliveries of bottles of milk.

mortified: Literally turned gangrenous. As used in Ulster, terribly embarrassed.

muirnin: Irish. Pronounced *moornyeen*. Darling.

National Health: The United Kingdom of which Northern Ireland is a part had universal state-funded health care for its citizens.

neat: Of spirits. Straight up.

nose out of joint: Angry.

no worries, she'll be right: Supreme Australian assurance that the outcome will be favourable.

Omadán: Irish. Pronounced *omadawn*. Male idiot.

operating theatre: OR.

Paddy hat: Soft-crowned tweed hat.

peat: Also known as turf. An accumulation of partially decayed compressed vegetable matter used in Ireland (and elsewhere) as fuel for fires.

petrol: Gasoline.

pew (have or take a): Bench in a church. (Please be seated.)

pip: Pit.

power cut: Power outage.

powerful: Very strong or large.
quare: Ulster and Dublin pronunciation of "queer," meaning "very" or "strange."
rasher: A slice of bacon for frying with an eye and a streaky tail, from the back of the pig.
rickets, taking the: Nothing to do with the vitamin D deficiency disease, but an expression of having had a great surprise or shock.
rightly (do): Very well. (Be adequate if not perfect for the task).
scuttered: Very drunk.
sent down: Expelled from university.
sister (nursing): In Ulster hospitals nuns at one time filled important nursing roles. They no longer do so except in some Catholic institutions. Their honorific, "sister," has been retained to signify a senior nursing rank. Ward sister: charge nurse. Sister tutor: senior nursing teacher. (Now also obsolete because nursing is a university course.) In North America the old rank was charge nurse or head nurse, now it's nursing team leader unless it has been changed again since I retired.
So/so it is, etc: Tacked to the end of a sentence for emphasis in County Cork/Ulster.
spailpin: Irish. Pronounced *spalpeen*. Rascal.
spondulix: Money.
surgery: What a North American physician would call the office.
take the light from your eyes: Absolutely amaze you.
tea (time): The main evening meal. (Time for).
that there/them there: That/them with emphasis.
thole: Put up with.
thran: Bloody minded.

tinnie: Tin. Australians frequently add "ie," as in "barbie" for barbeque.

too right: Australian for very true.

townland: A mediaeval geographic term encompassing a small village and the surrounding farms.

tumble dryer: Spin dryer.

two shakes of a duck's tail: Very quickly.

wean: Pronounced *wane.* Small child.

wee: Small, but in Ulster can be used to modify almost anything without reference to size. A barmaid, an old friend, greeted me by saying, "Come in, Pat. Have a wee seat and I'll get you a wee menu, and would you like a wee drink while you're waiting?"

wee man (in the name of): Devil. (In the devil's name.) Expression of surprise.

wheeker: Absolutely marvelous.

windscreen wiper: Windshield wiper.

wise woman: Herbalist, keeper of traditional lore, and often believed to have supernatural power.